PUFFIN BOOKS

Editor: Kaye Webb

BREAD AND HONEY

Anzac Day was never just an ordinary holiday without school in Michael Cameron's house. Grandma was always up late the night before making a wreath of chrysanthemums – green for ten million heroes, white for sorrows, red for love – to place at the foot of the War Memorial in Main Street, after the sound of drums and marching men and medals jingling had died away.

For 13-year-old Michael, unsure of himself, lonely since his troubles with the Farlows who lived next door, confused by the conflicts in his own family and in the world about him, this particular Anzac morning is to prove more important than any other he has known, even though he misses the parade, and only hears the drums and trumpets in the distance.

Because of his meeting with Margaret, on the rain-swept seashore beyond the tea-tree scrub, and his subsequent dramatic encounter with Bully Boy MacBaren and Flackie, the bully's hanger-on, Michael finds, quite suddenly, that some of his confusion is resolved, that he can begin to look for his own answers to the problems and the conflict in his world.

For readers of eleven and over.

Bread and Honey won the Australian Children's Book of the Year Award for 1970.

Cover design by Con Aslanis

Ivan Southall

Bread and Honey

Penguin Books

Penguin Books Ltd, Harmondsworth,
Middlesex, England
Penguin Books Australia Ltd, Ringwood,
Victoria, Australia

First published by Angus & Robertson 1970
Published in Puffin Books 1972
Copyright © Ivan Southall, 1970

Printed in Australia for
Penguin Books Australia Ltd
at Halstead Press, Sydney

CHAPTER ONE

At 7.30, or thereabouts, Michael's eyes opened and he sat up with a start that left him sick in the stomach. What on earth was he doing in bed when he should have been rushing like mad for the bus stop with schoolbag flying high and cap held hard to his head?

'Blooming Grandma,' he wailed. 'Slept in again!'

He could almost hear that bus roaring away, could almost see himself racing after it, leaping up and down, yelling, 'Hey, hey!' The things that happened to Michael Cameron wouldn't happen to a dog.

Eight miles to the railway station and the train gone, clackety-clacking up to town. Two hours late for school by the time the next bus came around.

'Not again, Cameron,' his form master would sigh.

He would lose points for his House because punctuality was *compulsory* at his school—like winning at games. They were always telling the kids that losing was good for the character, which should have made Michael a saint! But they didn't give points for coming last and took them away for coming late. Michael's score was already about minus forty-eight. The kids would glare while he stammered to explain that it was *difficult* when Dad was away. . . . He was panicking stark naked round the bedroom with his pyjamas thrown off into a heap, bellowing for Grandma. 'Where's my shirt? Where's my suit? Golly, Grandma, we've slept in again.'

Then he stopped and looked at himself with surprise

and smiled, and scratched himself gleefully, and thumbed his nose at all the kids in class who had called him a crumb when he wasn't a crumb at all. 'You shouldn't be there yourselves,' he scoffed, 'you silly lot of clowns. There's no school today. It's Anzac Day. You should have stayed at home.'

Suddenly, he didn't feel sick any more—felt very cheeky indeed—and listened for Grandma with a cocked ear, but she had not made a move. Grandma could turn the world on or off as she chose. When she took out her hearing aid she retreated into a silent place where clocks didn't strike and people's mouths were holes that didn't make sounds. 'One of the consolations,' Grandma said, 'of being old.' But it drove everyone else mad. Dad would roar at her, 'Switch it on, Mother. For pity's sake!'

It was quieter than a Sunday outside, and grey. Fine misty rain was out there, trees were drooping, puddles lay on the straight path to the gate, puddles for splashing in if a fellow weren't supposed to be half a man—the half that was expected to behave, of course, not the half that could do as it pleased.

Anzac Day.

Not exactly an ordinary holiday without school in Michael's house. Grandma was up late as a rule the night before making a wreath of chrysanthemums, Grandma with age-freckled hands at the kitchen table weaving stems through leaves and flowers, green for heroes, white for sorrows, red for love. There she would sit for hours, dry-eyed, weaving flowers to place at the foot of the War Memorial in Main Street early during the morning of Anzac Day—after the sound of drums and marching men and medals jangling had died away. That huge crowd of people standing round; Grandma, wreath in hand, waiting her turn; Dad never there. Michael once with a breathless feeling and a big question

2

that he suddenly had to ask. The moment flashed across his mind.

'Grandma!'

'Shhhh.'

'But, Grandma!'

'Wait until afterwards, dear.'

Her hand had closed over his shoulder giving it a squeeze. He had been smaller then. What was the question that had been so terribly important? How could he forget a question so important that he had wanted to blurt it out and break the silence as wreath after wreath was placed on the ground? Was it last year? Was it the year before? Grandma had taken him to the Anzac parade so many times.

He murmured, a little uncomfortably, as he sometimes did when he embarrassed himself, and sniffed loudly to put it out of his thoughts and rubbed hard at his empty stomach that was flatter than a board and decided that it was not really cold out there this morning.

The grey light had a heavy look about it, as though heavy with interesting smells of earth and sea, as though trees and plants and blades of grass couldn't bear the weight without bending, a *prehistoric* light, with cave-men dragging home their girlfriends by the hair of their heads and sabre-toothed tigers licking their chops and kids like Michael not having to wear clothes.

That was a much more comfortable thought, and he recognized it as perhaps a sign of another of those surprising days when sight and hearing and feeling and touch wound up like a very tight spring and everything in the world belonged to him. If he had scrambled into his clothes and headed for the breakfast table or raced for the bus he would have gone rushing on into the day not knowing it was there. But he was naked and beautiful clean air brushed over him—like feathers dipped in dew! Emu feathers? Big and fluffy. All dewy.

3

He edged to the mirror and expanded his chest until his ribs almost cracked. 'Not bad,' he thought, and inspected himself from several interesting angles, flexing his muscles and posing, and saw a stunning-looking fellow on the cover of a health magazine, with the face of Michael Cameron, a chest of about fifty inches and a weeny waist and a purple sash across a mighty shoulder bearing the words *Mr Universe*. When he looked a bit harder it was only the ordinary Michael in the shadows of the mirror, bones and all.

A shower would be super this morning. Dad wasn't home to hurry him out of it and Grandma was dead to the world. A fellow could stand there for as long as he liked while water pelted down and steam became a cloud misting on the white mosaic tiles, dripping in dribbles from the wall, billowing out of the open window. Different from other days when he had to stand there just to get clean. He could never fathom that; lying in bed doing nothing all night but having to wash the dirt off in the morning. 'What dirt, Dad? Here, sniff under me arm. I'm as sweet as a nut.'

He heaved the window up, grating it as far as it would go, and wet air flowed in off the long limp grass. Who wanted showers of soap and steam? Boy, he'd love to run out there and roll in the rain!

Over and over, rolling in the rain. . . .

But he didn't dare. She'd see, as she had seen before. Mrs Farlow next door would say, as she had said six months ago, 'Disgusting.' Then probably she would add, whether it was true or not: 'and in front of Jillian! He's without shame.'

Michael wrinkled his nose. What was disgusting about it? The world fairly creaked with bodies, thousands of millions of them, half of them of one kind and half of the other. Everybody knew what everybody else had. It was a mystery the way grown-ups carried on, as if a

4

body was something you were supposed not to have. And who was Jillian anyway? A crummy little kid not twelve years old with nothing better to do with her time than spy.

'It's not to happen again, Dr Cameron,' Mrs Farlow had said. 'I warn you. It's not good enough any more. He's not a baby now. There's something wrong with that boy.'

Michael had heard through the wall. Golly, it was a row. Dad being awfully matter-of-fact for a while, as if discussing the weather, but Mrs Farlow performing like a *prima donna*. That was what Dad said to her when he lost his temper. 'It's not an opera, Mrs Farlow. You're not a *prima donna*, Mrs Farlow. I'll not have him spoken of in these terms. There's something wrong with *you*, Mrs Farlow.'

Good old Dad.

Michael sneered across the garden at a glimpse of the Farlow's fence, at the one new paling about six months old that Mrs Farlow, her very own self, had slapped into place and hammered home, bending all the nails of course, just to make the men feel bad. Michael had heard Mr Farlow complain, 'If you'll give the hammer to me, woman, I'll do it. You're making yourself ridiculous.'

Dad hadn't said anything for a few days; that was Dad's style. His punishments didn't take the form of hidings, but hung over the landscape, threatening, like storms not sure when to break. 'Michael,' he had grumbled at last. It was always *Michael* in that particular tone when a lecture was coming. 'You're growing up. You're a big boy.'

Dad had scratched at the top of his head and tugged at his greying hair; that was reckless of him. Dad was getting a bit thin up there. 'Look here. Surely you realize we don't wear clothes only to keep warm. Mrs

Farlow's right, up to a point. No one cared when you were four or five but you're a big boy now. You know what I've told you about life; I've not left you ignorant or muddied by the dirt you dig up behind the shelter-sheds at school. You've got to start behaving responsibly. Men and women have been wearing clothes for thousands of years because we have learnt that it is best for all of us; nothing to do with what's right or wrong. These nudists—I can't work them out; it's not like that for most of us. Perhaps girls can get excited and not show it, but that's not the way it is for boys. When we clothe ourselves modestly we start creating. Would you rather live in a house like this or under a slab of rock? You touch a switch and cook your dinner. Turn a tap and shower in hot water. Twist a knob and a picture of the world is in your living-room. Open a book and a miracle of imagination is yours for the reading. Drop a sapphire on a plastic disk and listen to the most wonderful sounds any creature has heard. The rain falls and you don't get wet. You're safe. In my opinion, boy, men and women have done this for themselves because some enterprising fellow with more than one thought on his mind had the sense to hang a strip of bark across his middle—*not* because he was cold. You remember that, Michael, or I'll string you up by the toes.'

So when it got down to brass tacks, Dad was the same as the rest of them. Laying down the law; hammering the point. He was on their side and didn't understand. A fellow didn't want to run around naked all the time showing off what he had. The thought was never even there until they started screaming about it and making an issue of it. Didn't they know it was like an itch or a kick at a football? Just happened once in a while, sometimes when you felt like it, other times by surprise. Dad took things too far; talk of sapphires and cooking the dinner had as much to do with rolling in the grass

6

as the price of fish. And grown-ups weren't too bad at stripping off either; maybe they reckoned it was different when the temperature was ninety in the shade and a hundred thousand baked side by side in the sun on the sand. Different for *them*.

All those horrible-looking bodies; all lumps and bumps and blotches and hairy legs lined up in rows, only the young ones looking nice. Mrs Farlow in a swim-suit was the last straw—'Enough to put you off food for the rest of your days—' Dad's very own words.

All the art galleries, filled with paintings and statues on view all the time. People could stand and stare for as long as they pleased. They took you with the school and *made* you stare. But if Michael Cameron rolled on his own front lawn he was committing a crime. Whose fault was it if crummy Jillian Farlow had her nose pressed to the crack in the fence? His or hers? She'd get her nose stuck there one of these days and they'd have to prise her out with a crowbar.

He murmured again, uncomfortably, and was cross with himself for allowing his thoughts to go in the direction that made him miserable. There was a nice warm, happy feeling down deep and he wanted it to bubble up and take charge, but all sorts of things kept getting in the way, and when half of him wanted to head for the bathroom the other half stayed exactly where it was, stretching in that cool current of light and air, daring the world to look in on him, daring Grandma to walk in and say, 'Godfathers, boy. Cover yourself in front of the window. That's rude.' But Grandma didn't come and no one walked by. Maybe Grandma wouldn't have cared anyway. She was funny. *Terribly* old-fashioned, yet she'd barge in on him in the bathroom as if he weren't there.

It was very quiet outside, deathly quiet except for the dripping of the rain. Trees and grass and greenygreyness and somewhere, over the edge of the cliff, the sea lying like lead, solid and silent. The temptation was awful. He'd love to slide over the window-sill and run all the way to the sea and swim for miles, out past the sand bars, out into the channel where the big ships steamed, the cargo ships, the liners, the grey ships with guns.

Once upon a time, Dad said, ten million men marched to war to have their heads blown off. Once a year on Anzac Day, Dad said, everybody thought about it, perhaps for an hour, at least for a minute, and shops and offices and factories didn't open and schools stayed shut and almost everyone slept in. Dad, when he was home, slept in too. But Dad hadn't come home during the night; the inside of the house had that dead feeling. When Dad was there it felt alive. And Michael's brothers weren't there either, though he didn't care much about them. He thought of Richard the physicist working with his rockets hundreds of miles away, and of Gregory the metallurgist working with his bauxite even farther away. Other kids had boys for brothers; Michael's brothers were men. Terribly condescending, patting him on the head, slinging him a dollar to spend, but never rolling up their sleeves for a bit of fun. They never wrote while they were away, and, like Dad, would have slept in on Anzac Day if they had been at home.

Dad wouldn't go to the march with Grandma even though he had medals from the war in a drawer of his desk.

'All that's over, Mother,' Michael had heard him say. 'I don't want to remember that I bombed Dresden. If you had been there you wouldn't want to remember either.'

'You're wrong, you're wrong,' Grandma had cried. 'We don't go to the march to celebrate deeds. We go to *mourn* them. Haven't you any respect for the dead? For your own dead? For your own family?'

'Yes,' Dad had said, 'too much respect to wear it on my sleeve in public.'

'If that's the way you feel you should resign from your job. Taking money from the Government, if that's the way you feel, is a sin. How can you possibly believe in your job? You're dishonest. You're immoral. You're a fraud.'

It was hard trying to understand what was what when Dad and Grandma got together. They loved each other an awful lot but couldn't agree on anything. All the time arguing or observing a cool silence or speaking to each other round corners: 'Michael, tell your father. . . .' 'Michael, tell your grandmother. . . .' There was nothing about being stupid that kids could show *them*. Yet Grandma was a very dignified old lady of eighty-three, and Dad was a scientist whose opinions were so important that the Prime Minister called him on the telephone.

'We're not fighting, Michael,' Grandma would say. 'Don't get the wrong idea. It's really only a game.'

Suddenly, the cold quarry tiles of the veranda were slapping under his feet and he was leaping in the air and rolling in the grass.

Rolling over and over in the rain, driving out all the thoughts and unhappy feelings he didn't want, then lying still, as still as a frog wrapped in grass, listening, smiling, heart thudding like the Salvation Army Band marching down Main Street on Anzac Day, out in front of all the men who fought in the wars; thud, thud, thudding on the drums. Even shivering deliciously with nerves because it was not like being down on Deakin Beach after dark. There was a danger here that was hardly ever there; Grandma's window not fifteen feet away, the Farlow's fence not twenty feet away, the street not sixty feet away. *Anyone* could walk by; *anyone* could see. It was like hanging by the finger-tips over a hundred foot drop.

But there were no footsteps, no voices, no sounds of people. Grandma didn't beat on her window-pane, Jillian didn't snigger from beyond the fence. He sank into the grass, down and down, and rain pattered on his back, and his nerve-ends stood up to meet it, to coax it into trickles, to wriggle it into pools. He had to clench his teeth from the agony and the joy.

He rolled again, over and over, and rocked from side to side and allowed the world to rain gently on the front of him. He stuck out his tongue to lap it up. He wriggled and sank down.

'The earth is a practical place, Michael,' Dad had been saying from way back. 'Head out of the clouds, son. Face facts.' Other kids had believed in Santa Claus; other kids had put their baby teeth in tumblers of water and fairies had passed by with wands and changed them into shining silver coins. 'Don't put your faith, my boy, in silly imaginations. There are no fairies, no ghosts, no magicians, no angels with harps. There are no mysteries in heaven or earth that can't be expressed mathematically as formulae or dismissed as poisonous nonsense. You accept the world for what it is. The rock that hangs on the cliff is hard; you can analyse it, you can break it down into invisible particles; but when that rock falls and hits you on the head it kills you dead. That's life, my boy. That's nature. Blood and claw. Your Grandma tells you it's God who's good and man who's bad. If God is good He's got a lot to answer for!'

Dad talked too much.

'Your father,' Grandma said, 'is godless. He breaks my heart. Only forty years ago he was a boy like you. What those forty years have done! He's forgotten what it's like to be a boy. You must be different from the rest, Michael.

For your mother's sake let's have one like her, to rest her soul in peace. *Believe* in things, Michael. It doesn't matter if you're wrong. I don't care what your father says. Santa Claus *did* come down the chimney.'

Grandma also talked too much. It was a family failing.

The world rained gently on him. There weren't any famines or earthquakes or storms. There wasn't any blood. There weren't any claws. It was a gentle world. There were tiny insects and coolness and coldness and grass and he pressed his face against the earth and listened to a very deep distance—a dark, throbbing distance like kneeling beside the bed with Grandma in the background. He tried to block the thought off, but it had come, it was there. Grandma as ancient as papyrus, breathing breath a century old, insisting upon a 'quiet time with God'.

'Say your prayers, Michael.'

So he'd say God look after this and God look after that; but if He was God why did He have to be told by a boy? But he'd mumble on for a minute or two because Grandma went for mumbles in a big way. Dad said that Grandma associated pure and lofty thoughts with words that people couldn't hear properly in church and that she, personally, couldn't hear at all because they were beyond the range of her hearing aid.

'When Grandma was a little girl, my boy, Britannia ruled the waves and things were different then. People were different. The world was different. Millions of children all over the world kneeling beside millions of beds mumbling millions of words. The noise in heaven must have been deafening. God didn't hear a word, unless he thought they were asking for a great noise and so gave them jet engines, atom bombs and wars.'

So he'd try to think of this God clanging at an anvil striking stars and cooking up planets in thumping great urns. He'd try to think of Him *everywhere*, as Grandma said, and He would get so huge He had no shape at all. He'd be like jelly or fog or scrambled radio waves.

Or was He the rain lying in a pool in the small of his back that flowed like a river between hills when he wriggled his bottom? Or was He that huge silence made bigger by dripping sounds and bird sounds and people asleep in bed? Made bigger still by the oily presence of the sea imagined at the foot of the cliffs like something that might slide off the edge of the earth and slip into space, a vast, sliding, undulating slab of silence falling over and over in space?

Goodness!

What about Deakin Beach after dark? Terrific. Starlight and black space and sand and lapping water and the great looming crescent of the cliff. Down there he was alone on the earth and he could slide into the sea and lie head above water if people from other planets came by. Which they hardly ever did. Fellows smooching along with their girls, saying the drippiest things. Men weaving along with their dogs, stumbling in the dark.

Once Ray Farlow had come creeping along the edge, calling in a hoarse whisper.

Michael scowled at the Farlow's fence. He didn't want to think of Ray coming along the water's edge, calling.

'I know you're there, Mick. Where are you, Mick?'

Ray had come wading out.

'Where are you, Mick? I can't see you.'

They had grown up in houses side by side. They had gone to the same school to the Sixth Grade. There was nothing in the world they hadn't talked about, practically nothing they hadn't done together, hardly a secret not shared, scarcely ever a squabble. Ray should have been his brother, then nothing would have gone wrong.

Ray had come wading into the water after dark and he had never done that before. His Mum didn't allow him out alone after dark; Michael's Dad imposed the same rule, but Dad had been in America then and Grandma had nodded off to sleep in a chair as she often did.

'Hey, Mick!'

It was funny the way he had felt, sort of embarrassed, because all his clothes were hidden under the cliff, and he had never felt quite like it in his life. He had taken fright and somehow sunk to the bottom and drifted there, bumping about like a dead body. Deakin Beach after dark was the *one* secret he wouldn't share. In twelve years they had never met on the beach after dark, except with their families on hot nights or for hilarious cricket on the sand with a herd of summer kids in bright moonlight.

Suddenly, Ray's hands had snatched at his legs and Michael in fright had struggled wildly and brought Ray down in a crash of foam. Ray had shrieked, 'You silly so-and-so. I thought you were drowned.' Then he had struggled to his feet, fully clothed except for shoes and socks, drenched to the skin. 'Strike me,' he had wailed. 'Mum'll murder me. How am I going to get my clothes dry? How am I going to explain?' Then he had seemed to loom closer and his voice had altered, had sounded almost hurt. 'Gee, Mick.... What are you doing like that?'

'Like what? What are you talking about?'

But Ray had gone quiet.

'Did you come down here to catch me out or something? Like peeping through a keyhole or something?'

Ray had waded ashore, shaking himself like a puppy.

'Golly, Ray.'

But Ray wouldn't say a thing and from that moment they had grown apart. It was a shame. Ray must have thought the same way as his Mum.

It was cold lying in the rain and Michael wished he had not come out of doors. *To roll in the grass!* What was he trying to do? Get himself locked in gaol?

He scuttled to the house and crept along the veranda, trailing wet footmarks and black mud and bits of autumn leaves, and sidled over the window-sill, back inside. There he shuddered and hurriedly shut the window and drew the curtains and discovered he was shivering uncontrollably, with shakes to his fingertips and chattering teeth. If goose pimples were a dollar a dozen he'd be a millionaire. What a stupid thought! He threw his arms across himself, beating at his shoulders with the flat of his hands, and danced on the spot to try to get warm, but resisting the temptation to part the curtains again to make certain that no one had seen. Somehow, he thought he'd rather not know. If the Farlows were up! If the Farlows had seen! His mind boggled; for two pins he would have hidden under the bed.

Mrs Farlow was right, of course. Something was wrong with him. Only a nut would rush out there and roll in the grass. He was *stinging* all over, great streaks of black sandy mud on his body, bits of grass and the pollen of weed flowers stuck to him. What a mess. What a proper nut. Irritably, he dragged the cover from the bed and threw it over his shoulders like a gown and shook fiercely within it, trying to order himself to be still, puffing hot air from inside him over his lips and cheeks and nose with the most extraordinary twists of his mouth.

'I'm crazy,' he said. 'Stark, staring.'

But no one came. No one knocked at the front door. The telephone didn't ring. Grandma didn't shuffle into the room with a troubled frown. *Nothing happened.*

He had got away with it.

The shivering stopped and he edged across to the mirror again and a scraggy-looking head with hair standing on end blinked back at him through the curtained gloom.

'Hi, Mick.'

'Hi, fella. How's yourself?'

14

It had been terrific out there. Puddles in the small of his back, rain drops spattering his chest, beading and glistening, the grey sky so low he had had to wriggle under it.

Everything was quiet again; even his pulse had stopped thundering in his head. And it was Anzac Day. He giggled. Poor old Grandma. If she had seen him out there what *would* she have said?

He'd go to the march with Grandma, all prim and proper, trying to look grave, trying to feel sad, trying to think about the dead men. Time for Grandma to be getting out of bed, lazy old woman. It was hard trying to think of men who were dead before you were born. What were they like then? Different? Did they like rolling in the grass? Grandma had been young then, younger anyway. Fancy Grandma being young. She *never* could have been. Fancy Grandma rolling in the grass!

What about those fellows waving their guns and hissing through their teeth, lips drawn back; really hissing, maybe because they were scared, climbing dirty great cliffs or splicing the mainbrace or looping the loop? Making battle cries, *Waaaahhh*, or something like that. Ten million fellows marching to war to have their heads blown off. Fellows on their bellies creeping round corners with knives in their teeth and machine-guns at the ready. Fellows getting shot at dawn or sunk in ships or screaming crunch into the earth in power dives and smoke. They had faces he couldn't quite think up, like photographs in other people's houses.

'Hey, Grandma. Are you awake? Time to be getting ready for the march.'

Grandma was asleep and her room smelt like a cave. She hated fresh air; she reckoned it was for birds and for pumping up tyres. Her hearing aid was on the bedside table. There was a tumbler of water, too, with her teeth in it, but not for turning into silver coins. He wished she'd hide them somewhere instead of leaving them around, leering.

'It's ten minutes to eight, Gran. The march is at nine. What about some breakfast, Gran?'

She didn't sleep much, of course, or that was what she said. Just an hour or two here and there. The rest of her life she spent wide awake, aching from tiredness. She always reckoned she could never get to sleep until six o'clock in the morning.

'Come on, Gran. Shake a leg.'

She had lost her husband in the First World War, two sons in the Second World War, and a grandson was still in hospital from something that had happened in Vietnam years ago. Anzac Day must have been a *horrible* day for her, when he came to think of it. He had a rough idea of the sort of pain it added up to because of Mum dying and all. He almost put a hand to her, to waken her, but remembered the bed cover over his shoulders and his naked self underneath.

'Gran!'

The clocks ticked, loudly, but everything else was silent. Everything had an empty sort of smell. And it wasn't only Grandma lying in bed like a shell. The emptiness was always there until Dad's tobacco smoke filled it up. Irish stuff. Smelt like fruit and drifted in layers like cirrus cloud throughout the house, particularly when the sun was shining in the windows.

'Fairies, Daddy. Look!' How long ago was it that he had said that?

'No, Michael. Not fairies. Tobacco smoke.'

Dad was very scientific. Very exact. It was frustrating at times, always having to be so *exact*. Every item of news he brought home from school, every story he told about things that happened, had to be *exact*. Ruined half the news; spoilt half the stories. It was fun exaggerating a bit. But it was dreary when Dad was away.

He dressed over the top of the mud and the wet and the pollen and the grass. He thought about washing it off, but then deliberately dressed; the idea of a shower seemed wrong somehow. It had been terrific out there on the grass; how could he wash *that* off? Like washing something sacred off. It was a fact; a fellow washed half his life down the sink: every game he ever played, nosebleeds, hours of sleep, bread and honey, sweat, inky fingers—washed them all down the sink. Swirled them down the plug hole into the earth and then forgot.

CHAPTER TWO

A head looked round Ray's door for a moment or two.
It was Mum. 'Your father's out of the bathroom, dear.
Breakfast soon.' She looked pretty good in her Red Cross
uniform with her extra special bit of ribbon and the
medal hanging there that the Governor had given her
for helping people.

'Mum,' he yelled after her, 'is it raining?'

'Yes, dear, I'm afraid so.'

'Blow.'

Mum came back. 'Warm underclothes, Ray.'

'Yeh, I know. Blooming rain. What'd it have to rain
today for?'

'Up you get. We don't want to be late.'

'You look beaut, Mum.'

'Do I?' She seemed frankly surprised. 'Well, that's
very nice, dear. You've made my day. But it doesn't give
you the right to stay in bed. You know how your father
hates delay. Don't antagonize him this morning.' Mum
had a tone in her voice that sounded interesting.

'What's on, Mum?'

'What do you mean, *what's on*? The march, of course.'

Ray gave her a conspiratorial look. Mum was hopeless.
'What else, Mum?'

'Nothing, dear. Why should there be?' But she moved
quickly from the doorway, as if getting out of danger.
Mum was funny. Any secret entrusted to her was as
good as lost; the atmosphere of the house would change.
She'd start glancing at Dad from the corner of her eyes,

she'd dance her fingertips along the edges of tables and chairs, she'd dip her head in a 'little-girl' way. Mum liked to share everything, her pleasures as well as her troubles, and *everyone* would know that exciting news was about to break as soon as Dad got round to it. Sometimes he was so slow that Mum would heave a sigh: 'Please, Jack, *do* tell them or I think they'll die.' She meant, of course, that *she'd* die.

What could happen on Anzac Day apart from the march, which was always rather beaut, and the service at the War Memorial, and lemonade and cakes in the hall afterwards? Nothing. Except that Dad would come home by taxi late at night, about half-past eleven or twelve, singing songs and stumbling round the place a bit. That seemed to be Dad's privilege once a year; like Mum with her Conference each July, being away for a whole weekend, and like the kids having Christmas and belly-aches from eating too much.

Dad always got a bit merry on Anzac Day from drinking too many beers with his old soldier mates. Early to bed was the rule on Anzac night. Of course, Mum was only getting Jillian and him out of the way, trying to fool herself that they'd be sound asleep before Dad came in so that he wouldn't be embarrassed next morning. Dad was not a drinking man, not really, never got properly drunk at any time, just a bit merry on Anzac Day. Mum was always very gentle, didn't get cross with him, didn't shout. What she really said to him Ray didn't know. She always spoke so quietly, always handled him so well, then the bedroom door at the front of the house would shut and for a while Dad would laugh and giggle in a silly boyish way as if everything in the world was a great big joke.

'Ray! Bathroom!'

'Yeh, Mum. I'm there.'

He scuttled from his room to make good his word

19

and crashed into Jillian in the hall. She had been preening herself in front of the big bronzed mirror there. 'Clumsy,' she hissed. 'Look where you're going, why don't you?'

He was vaguely aware of her Girl Guide uniform, crisp and smart. He pulled a face at her and darted into the bathroom.

'Mum,' she wailed, 'he's not in the bathroom. He's running round the house. Mum, he poked out his tongue at me.'

'Ray,' Dad boomed. 'If you're not in the bathroom, where are you?'

'*I am in the bathroom.*'

'He's not. He's running round the house. He crashed straight into me. He's winded me, he has. He's not allowed to run round the house.'

'No, no, no, of course he's not.' Dad came lumbering to the front bedroom door, buttoning his shirt. 'Get out from under people's feet, Jillian. Your dressing-table's the proper place for looking at yourself.'

'Jack,' Mum called, 'bacon or chops?'

'Ray,' Dad demanded, '*are* you in that bathroom or not?'

Ray had the shower taps running hot, belching steam for dramatic effect. He poked a toothbrush in his mouth, snatched a towel and reeled into the hall. 'Can't a fellow have a wash? What's going on?'

'Were you running through the house?'

'Me? Fair go. I'm in the bathroom, Dad.'

'Jack, do you want bacon or chops?'

'He poked his tongue out! He nearly knocked me flat!'

'I did not!'

'Ray,' Mum called, 'don't waste hot water, dear. Do get on with your shower. Jillian, I could do with some help in the kitchen. Jack, did you hear me—bacon or chops?'

'Chops!' Dad bellowed and vanished from the doorway, and Jillian stood resentfully alone, wondering why it was that the innocent party should collect the abuse. Her hands went to her hips and she tossed hair from her eyes and stalked to the kitchen.

'Ray's a pig,' she said.

'Give the porridge a stir, dear.'

'Yuk,' shuddered Jillian. 'Porridge!'

'Then set out the table. Put out the grapefruit spoons. Special treat this morning.'

'Grapefruit! Yuk!'

'I wouldn't say that, dear. Not at ten cents each.'

Jillian stirred furiously at the porridge. 'He crashed into me, he did. I hate him. He *was* running round the house.'

'You know that, dear, and I know, but we don't want Dad upset, do we?'

'Just because it's Anzac Day?'

Mum danced her fingers along the top of the refrigerator. 'Yes, I suppose so.'

'Doris,' Dad bellowed, 'where's my regimental tie?'

'Folded, dear, in the top pocket of your suit.'

'How many times have I told you not to fold my ties?'

'Oh my goodness,' breathed Mum, 'I wish I didn't forget.' And like a little girl turned up the whites of her eyes at Jillian. 'Sorry, dear,' she called, 'but your suit's pressed and your medals are polished and your shoes are cleaned.'

'All right, all right, I take it back. You're a marvellous wife. I'll bring myself out and you can scratch my neck.'

Jillian paused over the cutlery drawer, shaking her head, confused, feeling a little lost. So much went on between Mum and Dad that was beyond her understanding.

'Have you got the grapefruit spoons, dear?'

'Yes, Mum.'

Then Mum whispered, 'Dad's going to make it a family day. Just the four of us. It's a secret.'

'Isn't he going to get drunk tonight?'

'Jillian!' She looked absolutely shocked. 'What a horrible thing to say—about *that* man.'

Jillian wanted to cry. She had not meant to say it; it had come out.

'You're lucky to have a father like him.'

'Did I say I wasn't?'

'Don't ever let me hear that word from you again. Your father has never drunk to excess in his life. Your father was an officer and a gentleman and he still is.'

Jillian's lip was quivering and tears were showing.

'All right, Mum. Don't carry on. I'm sorry.'

'I hope so—and you'd better cheer yourself up a bit. A face like bad news all the time. What's got into you this morning?'

Jillian turned away. 'Nothing.'

'I don't believe that. What's the trouble?'

'My uniform . . . no one cares. . . .' Jillian gave a sob. 'You haven't even said it looks nice. You haven't even noticed. And Ray crashed into me and didn't even see. First time I've ever worn my uniform. . . .'

'Oh, darling, don't be silly.' Mum's arms came round her and hugged her tight. 'Of course I've noticed. You look lovely.'

'I don't . . . you didn't say. . . . I'm ugly, I'm ugly all the time.'

'Oh, my sweet, what a thing to say. You're the prettiest girl in miles. I had things on my mind. Dad's got such good news for us. We're going to see the big match. Dad's driving us up after the march. We're going to see the charity match, the *big* football game, darling. Then we're going to dinner at a city restaurant afterwards. Your Dad's not done that in years, not since you were a baby. Don't let anything spoil our day, darling, not for us, not for him. It's costing him such a lot of hard-earned money. Come on: big smile. And when he tells you, *look surprised*.'

Jillian sniffed and felt surprised already. There was always such a fuss about Anzac Day being Dad's day. 'And he'll miss his party? He's not going off with the old soldiers?'

Mum smiled. 'He's a good man, your Dad. He gives up things for you children all the time.' Then she added, 'For me, too, I suppose.'

Jillian saw where Mum was looking, through the window, across the fence, to the Cameron house next door. There seemed to be a shadow for a moment, a passing change of expression in her eyes, and something of the shadow hit Jillian. There was a sudden, sharp ache inside.

Mum didn't seem to care for the Camerons, but Michael was nice. Jillian was sad that Michael didn't come to play with Ray any more. They were getting too big for games, Mum said, and Michael went to a posh private school anyway and had new friends now. Mum didn't like to discuss the Camerons.

She was turning the chops and they were spitting like fire-crackers in the pan.

Michael poured a tall glass of orange juice from a can and tipped cold milk on a large serving of crackly breakfast cereal, added a scoop of ice-cream, sliced a banana into it, scattered sticky rich brown sugar over it, added a quarter of a bottle of cream and a sprinkling of chocolate malted milk powder, and put three glazed cherries on top. It looked magnificent and he walked round it two or three times admiring it from different angles, clicking his tongue in appreciation. 'By crikey, what a sight. That's really somethin'.'

The big table stood in an alcove with dozens of small panes of glass, and curtains he could see through. They had been a large family once, or at least a family that liked room to spread. Mum used to set the table with silver for breakfast, used to be up an hour before anybody else getting things ready for the day. Sometimes she'd be out there in the garden, picking flowers with dew on them.

'Hey, Gran. Are you getting up or what?'

If Grandma had been sitting opposite she would have said, 'Say your grace, Michael.'

'Sure, Gran.'

Two, four, six, eight,
Bog in, don't wait.

He giggled. He had tried to pull it on Grandma once but she had had her hearing aid plugged in. She'd thrown a fit, but Dad had sat through it with a face so *straight*.

Mum used to put the dewy flowers with long stems on the table, not in a vase, just on the table.

Everything was very quiet. Grandma didn't come through the door twisting her jaws to rattle her teeth into place.

If she had been sitting at the table she might have said, 'Anzac Day is a time for tenderness, for remembering people you have loved. I feel no hate. How can you hate a German mother weeping for her son?'

Ten million fellows, Grandma, all marching towards each other hissing through their teeth. Their Mums should have said, you get lost, Mr Churchill; you boil your head, Mr Hitler; you go jump in the lake, Mr Roosevelt; you fight your own wars, Mr Stalin.

Yeh, Grandma; why didn't all the Mums say that?

If Dad had been at home he would have growled, 'The whole idea gives me a pain. It's worn out. Drums and medals and bugles. What do they want to drag it up out of the past for? I want to forget all about it.'

24

'Was it exciting, Dad? Did you see the bombs burst? Weaving through all the flak, Dad? Ray Farlow's Dad tells him how he won the Military Cross. By jimminy, it was terrific. He shot thirteen fellas with a machine-gun. He leapt into their hole and grabbed it off 'em. You don't tell me anything, Dad.'

Then Grandma would have said, suddenly forgetting herself, 'Godfathers, boy. What are you eating? You'll rot your boots.'

If Richard had been there he would have said, 'You must be firm, Father. You should not allow the kid to go to the march again. You're just standing by while he soaks up this old blood and glory stuff.'

To which Michael would have said, 'You're making rockets, aren't you? Making them and not caring who they hit. Who are you to talk?'

Yeh; that would have been telling him!

But nobody said anything. Nobody was there.

It was confusing. Dad hiding his medals but keeping a polish on them, Grandma saying she loved everything —but laying poison in the vegetable cupboard to kill the mice: 'Before they start breeding like rabbits. Filthy things.'

He peeled another banana.

Dad might have cut in, as he had done last year. 'If half the human race gets a kick out of butchering the other half, he's got to know about it. Don't you agree? Do you hide it from him? You're in missiles, Richard. Do you deceive yourself that they're for peaceful purposes? And what of Gregory's bauxite? Is it for sauce-pans?' Dad had huddled there, looking wretched. Michael had never seen him like that before. 'The old lady's right. Who am I to sound off? A defence adviser, telling governments which diabolical devices will kill the most soldiers for the least expenditure of money. He can go to the march with her; I see no reason why he shouldn't. Then he can judge for himself who is the more stupid or dishonest.'

That was the trouble; a fellow could never do anything for a nice simple reason, like *wanting* to do it, for instance. There always had to be a post-mortem. Why? Where? When? Other fathers just let their kids grow up and didn't interfere all the time. They might have slapped their kids around a bit, but who cared? Slaps landed on one ear and bounced off the other. Dad kept his hands to himself. Other people were the ones who knocked Michael around, people like prefects and sports-masters at school who reckoned that healthy boys were never found anywhere except in squads and teams. Or kids like Bully Boy MacBaren up the other end of town who was a blot on the earth. Bully Boy was a crumb. It seemed to be his special pleasure to pin Michael against a wall. One of these days he'd poke Bully Boy back, he'd hit him on the head with a brick. One of these days he'd get *real tough* with Bully Boy.

It was funny, wasn't it, that report from the headmaster lying in the drawer of Dad's desk. Dad shouldn't have left it around. He should have known a kid would go poking about when he was away from home. It was addressed to Dr G. D. Cameron. 'Confidential', it said. Blah, blah, blah, it read. 'Michael doesn't make friends as his brothers used to do. He won't assert himself. He lacks the competitive spirit. He is immature. He won't fight. His only conflict is with himself.' Michael knew it by heart, every word, and he got mad every time he thought about it. He didn't want to go to the rotten old school anyway. He'd rather have gone off to High School with Ray and the kids he knew. It was so far up to the city that by the time he got there and back home again the day was over. In the winter it was dark when he left in the morning and dark when he got back at night. Yet everyone reckoned it was a good school, even

Grandma, even Mrs Farlow. 'You're a very lucky boy,' Mrs Farlow said. 'I only wish we had the money to give Ray half the chance.'

His breakfast bowl was empty!

He stared in astonishment and could remember having eaten hardly any of it. 'I'll be jiggered. How could a fellow not taste *that*? Eat it and not taste it?' Then he groaned. It was like the school chaplain's heavy-handed stories with morals to them; you could see them coming a mile off. Eating ice-cream and not tasting it! Like getting nothing out of a school that was supposed to be terrific. He could almost hear the chaplain hammering the point home.

'Arrgh, nuts.' He tramped off to Grandma's bedroom to stir her up. She was still asleep, or seemed to be.

Was she dead?

The thought left him a bit sick. But she was breathing.

'Come on, Gran. Are you goin' to the march or aren't you? Wake up! The house could burn down and you wouldn't know.'

But she didn't twitch a sinew.

He stood there feeling helpless, wanting to shake her or shout against her ear. But she was as old as the earth. You had to treat things like Gran with respect.

'All right,' he grumbled, 'I'll go on my bloomin' own. I can't hang round here all day waiting for you to wake up. What do you want to sleep this morning for? You know I wanted to go to the march. There's no one else to go with.'

He wanted to go to feel sad; at that moment desired sadness more than anything, and gritted his teeth.

Mum was a face high up, looking down. From up there, too, a hand reached down, as cool as grass. He was about four and together they were walking over the rocks and the sea roared up. They were wet to the skin. They shrieked with laughter. Mum laughed down the years.

He could think of Mum right out there in the open on Anzac Day for everyone to see. He could even look like he was going to cry and no one minded. No one would say, to spoil it all, 'Cheer up, kid. It might never happen.' That was what Richard would have said. Richard was as hard as brass.

He slouched to the front door and kicked it. Outside it was still raining. He sat on the step and counted sixty-eight snails on the path. Stupid things they were. He'd have to crush the lives out of half of them to get to the gate. Which would die? Which would live? It was chance, wasn't it? Wherever his feet fell. 'Stupid snails,' he said. 'Don't you care if you die?'

Then he kicked with his heel viciously at the step, and ran through the grass and leapt the fence.

CHAPTER THREE

Suddenly, Michael was on the street. It was as if he had leapt onto a stage where another face was required. The polite face he would wear when people were around or when he went visiting with Grandma to suffer agonies of various kinds: 'Oh, no, Mrs Fitzsimmons, not for me, thank you. Not another slice of that super-dooper cake with real chocolate on the outside and real cream in the middle.'

He paused there, almost brushed his clothes down with his hands, almost smoothed his hair, but the street looked like death alley. He could have shot a cannon up the centre and winged not a bird. All the kids were indoors; all the oldies were asleep. Everything *dripped*. It looked grey and derelict, real droopy, like a street at the bottom of the sea.

In summer it was different. It would be roaring by this hour. All the summer-kids would be streaming to the beach from their holiday houses. The Lindens and Bischofs and the Olsens would be down from the city. Brian was a terrific kid; even his sister Wilma wasn't bad. Cars would be buzzing back and forth. Towels would be hung out to dry on every second tree. Mr Whippy would park his ice-cream van on the arch of th' cliff and play his tune. Yeh; but now it was like the grave and the summer crowd wouldn't be back for six or seven months.

He jumped for a crack in the pavement and landed fair and square, sighted another at a different angle and leapt again. From crack to crack like a ballet dancer with fine rain in his face and splashes in his hair from branches deliberately tugged and deliciously let go. Showers of autumn leaves and cool water. Heading for Main Street over the arch of the cliff, with arms swinging and legs swinging, along the road with a crest to it like the hump of a rainbow.

The sea over there was awfully quiet; not a sound from it, not a movement out there. There were glimpses through the tea-tree of a grey smudge where the horizon should have been. Had the sea really slipped over the edge of the world and gone sliding? Whooosh. Gone undulating into space like a slice of jelly? Passenger liners off to Mars, unexpectedly, and ocean-going whales in orbit squirting distress signals through their blow-holes; sea-bed dry; a fellow could walk to New Zealand.

The track to the cliff-face wound off through the tea-tree, wet and sandy black, and squealed like mice when he stepped on it. This was not the way to Main Street!

Sure. But it was early.

To Deakin Beach, the notice said, *193 Steps*, *Use With Caution*. They zigzagged all the way to the bottom. Feet flying on summer days, swinging round the corners. . . . Once he had taken off from two-thirds of the way down and tumbled head over side to the bottom. Mum fell from higher up.

'Be careful,' Grandma always said, 'remember your mother.'

But he was never careful. Would Mum have left a curse on the steps because she died there? Mum never cursed anything except for one stunning swear word screeched one day from the kitchen. Had she burnt herself? Had she dropped something? If he had ever known he had forgotten; he remembered only the word and her laughter afterwards. She had laughed for minutes.

The sea hadn't gone away. There it lay as though it had

run out of breath between storms. There was the beach down below sort of sidling into the sea, stirring the sea at the edges, drinking from it maybe, sipping. A slurping sound was there if he strained his ears until they almost split.

Anzac Day was a day for remembering.

Eleven steps from the top was where Mum had stopped climbing. She had been running with him, running up. 'I do feel funny, darling. Find Daddy.'

She had sagged against the rail, her face looking different. 'Hurry, darling.'

When they came back the rail was hanging by one nut and bolt, swinging like a pendulum.

It was hard trying to remember her now except when Dad showed his colour slides, life-size. Sometimes he took ages to change to the next picture. Gran would say, 'No more,' and perhaps leave the room.

Michael skipped down eleven steps, quickly, and held to the hand-rail of iron piping. When Mum had been alive it had been wood. Tea-tree and wire grass and fleshy-leaved succulents clung to the cliff face in crevices. There were neat holes where birds nested. He had scaled it once, barefoot, at a furious pace, farther around. It had crumbled beneath him, it had broken in his hands, stones dislodged had dropped as if falling into a pit without a bottom. But he had got home ahead of Bully Boy MacBaren. He had got inside and groaned against the door, shaking violently, and later washed his blood and dirt down the plug hole under the shower. Bully Boy didn't come often to Deakin Beach, even in summer.

Once summer was over not many people came at all and only the hottest days brought them out in autumn, then usually only the locals. Ray would come but Jillian hardly ever joined in anything. She was a sneaky kid with a dismal face. With a mother like hers it wasn't surprising. Ray said she was different at home but Michael didn't believe it. Ray was only trying to cover up for her; the kids reckoned that having a sister like her would be worse than having scarlet fever.

Bigger kids would come sometimes, strutting like turkeys, their girls swinging on their arms looking slinky, rubbing suntan oil into each other or kissing when they thought you weren't looking. They were stupid. 'Hi, Mick,' they'd say when he stopped to talk to them, but he knew they were wishing him to blazes. Sometimes he hid in the tea-tree or among the boulders and tossed pebbles at them, making them jittery. Sometimes he disguised his voice: 'When are you getting married, Peter Davies?' 'Hey! She's still in High School, Mister. Her dad'll chop your head off.'

In winter they came hardly ever.

Where did the lovebirds go in winter? He had asked Grandma but she had looked at him as if he had broken a window.

Winter was terrific. Then Deakin Beach was like his own backyard, as if he had bought it and had put fences up to discourage intruders. If he discovered footprints in the sand in winter he'd have a mystery that could start fantastic imaginings, like Adam discovering Eve or Crusoe discovering Friday or Darwin discovering evolution. This morning, the beach was as unmarked as on the day the world began.

He jumped eleven steps up, eleven jumps to the top, rain dribbling down his collar to his midriff.

It was a rare sort of morning; not what he had expected of it. It was going all peculiar. As if he was watching himself as others saw him, yet was able to hear the private thoughts of years tumbling in confusion. The way it was, as he had read, when a man's life 'flashed before his eyes' in the instant before death. Had Mum felt like this when she toppled over the cliff? Was this what they called a premonition? He pulled his hand sharply from the rail and stepped back, suddenly nervous and breathless and lonely. Suddenly wanting Mum very much.

Had she gone to Heaven? Grandma reckoned she had, but Dad would never give an opinion. You'd have thought he would have done, just for once. 'What I cannot prove, my boy, I cannot confirm. I would be deceiving you. What is Heaven but a question?' It wouldn't have hurt him to have spent a few days working on the formula; it couldn't have been harder than cracking problems for the government. 'All I know, Michael, that I can stake my life on, is that the earth is solid, the seas are liquid and the air is gas.'

What a horribly empty way of saying nothing.

Hundreds of years ago they could do better. Kids of thousands of years ago were luckier than that. The world was full of gods and demons and fairies then. They had answers for everything. Now even Grandma lost heart sometimes. 'It's your father and his science. I tell him it's wicked to destroy the things people believe in, but he's done it, he and others like him, and they think they're such clever fellows. Oh, Michael, I long for the days when I was ignorant, when childhood stories were the inspiration for grown-up people to live nobly. Men like your father have made a new world, but I know they'd have been better with the old one. These are bad times for grandmothers and children.'

He ran back to the road and tyres squealed on the wet bitumen, squealed on top of him, paralyzing him.

The wiper blades flicked back and forth and Mr and Mrs Farlow peered at him through the windscreen. He could have reached out a hand and leant on the mudguard. It was so close. He had nearly run under it. He saw Mrs Farlow sink back and Mr Farlow take his hands from the wheel and press them to his brow, then a rear window wound down and Ray poked his head out. 'What are you trying to do? Get yourself killed?'

Michael smiled thinly.

The front window wound down and Mrs Farlow said, 'Oh, Michael Cameron, what a stupid thing to do.'

He swallowed and stepped back into the gutter. 'I'm sorry, Mrs Farlow. . . .'

'Oh, Michael, if we'd killed you!' Then for a few moments she said nothing and with a sigh went on, 'What are you doing in the rain? What have you been doing at the beach at this hour?'

He was trembling too much to make proper explanations and felt too churned up to invent them. *Anyone* could have come by. Why did it have to be the Farlows?

Mr Farlow called, 'All right, Michael, no harm done, but watch your step!'

The car moved off and Ray yelled, 'See you, Mick.'

He nodded, overwhelmed by the feeling that the whole pattern of the morning could have been a premonition after all, could have been getting him ready to die. Didn't kids get killed every day?

The car was moving off. Jillian's face like a white mask was pressed to the rear window; so was Ray's, and he trailed after them, still trembling, for a time not realizing that they were coming back in reverse. He was surprised to see Ray's head and shoulders again stuck out in the rain. 'Where are you going, Mick? Are you going to the march?'

'Yeh.' He said it numbly, as if owning up to something dreadful.

'Why didn't you say so?'

'I didn't think. . . .'

'Well come on, do you want a ride or don't you?'

It was the last thing on earth he wanted; he felt so embarrassed with the Farlows.

Mrs Farlow was rapping on the glass with her knuckles. 'Michael!' She sounded sharp. 'For Heaven's sake get in out of the rain. Don't stand there.'

The door swung open for him, like the door of a cage. It was a foreign country in there, a gloomy place where everyone wore uniforms and belonged to things. Jillian was a Girl Guide, Ray was a Boy Scout, Mrs Farlow was a Red Cross something or other, Mr Farlow had a string of medals about a foot wide pinned to his overcoat. But Michael didn't belong to anything. Mrs Farlow's voice came out of the gloom like the voice of judgement. 'Your father, I suppose, is away?'

'Yes, Mrs Farlow.'

'Where is he this time?'

She made him feel guilty, as if Dad had robbed a bank or something and spent his time moving from hideout to hideout. 'In Canberra. . . .'

'Come on, boy! Jump in!' Mr Farlow reached an arm purposefully across to the open door, an arm like half a tree. His medals jangled like gipsy bangles. 'We're late enough now. Move over there, Jillian. Make room.'

'I've made room,' Jillian complained. 'It's Ray.' Her face, Michael noted, was as long as usual.

'Make more,' Ray grumbled. 'He's wet.'

'You could wring a bucket out of him,' said Mrs Farlow.

The man snorted. 'We'll all be wet before the morning's out. All he's got is a head start. Come on the pair of you, push up.'

Michael slid onto the seat and the door slammed. The car was still stale from being locked up in the garage all night, smelling of plastic seat covers and yesterday's cigarette smoke and Mrs Farlow's perfume. Michael's nose twitched and suddenly felt raw. It was the perfume that made him sneeze so unexpectedly that he didn't have time to smother it. 'I'm sorry,' he spluttered, gasping for breath, and Jillian seemed to glower at him and shrink into her corner. He glowered back. And Ray was looking at him as if he had smallpox. He wanted to get out again, but couldn't. He was trapped.

'Who's looking after you?' Mrs Farlow said.

'Grandma, of course.'

'I'm surprised, Michael. She sent you out on a morning like this dressed in shorts and shirt? Sneezing your head off!'

He shrugged, because he knew better than to argue with Mrs Farlow and at once sneezed again, heartily.

'Well, you're bound to die one way or the other,' Mrs Farlow said, 'under a car or from pneumonia. Jack, I think we should pull into the side of the road, empty him out, and send him home. It's absurd. The child should be in bed.'

'I'm not stopping.'

'Spraying his germs everywhere.'

'I'm not stopping.'

Her perfume smelt like moth-eaten furs stored in a cupboard and Michael's nose itched like mad; and that crummy Jillian had a look on her face like someone eating lemons. Ray was sitting up straight, sort of flinching, maybe trying to breathe through the other side of his neck.

Desperately Michael wrinkled his nose and his eyes smarted. He started shivering and it had nothing to do with cold.

'What were you doing down at the beach, Michael? Does your grandmother know you were there?'

'Huh?'

'The beach. What on earth did you go to the beach for on a morning like this? No overcoat. No cap. Short pants. You're old enough to know better than that. You're a big boy now.'

He grunted, breathlessly. They wouldn't understand if he told them. They wouldn't admit they understood if they did. They didn't want to like him any more; he knew that. It was a shame. It was like a foreign country, all right.

Ray said, 'We're all marching.'

'Are you?'

'Dad's leading this year. It's his turn. Your Dad never marches, does he? Why doesn't your Dad march, Mick?'

Michael felt impatient. 'Because he's got two wooden legs, he reckons.'

'Two ordinary legs, you mean. Two hairy ones. I've seen him in his shorts in the garden.'

He found himself looking at Jillian for no particular reason. 'It's special wood with hairs on.'

'That's enough,' said Mrs Farlow, rather tensely.

He sneezed and phlegm caught in his throat and he could hardly get his breath.

'Use your hanky, child, for *pity*'s sake.'

'I haven't got one.'

'You can have mine,' Ray said.

'He can't. You keep your handkerchief in your pocket.'

'Ray,' said Mr Farlow, surprisingly, 'I'm not sure that I approve of your remarks. If Dr Cameron chooses not to march it's his own business. Perhaps he's marching in Canberra, anyway.'

'He's not,' Michael said, 'because he's gone to see the Prime Minister. It's very important.'

'It must be,' Mrs Farlow said, 'if the Prime Minister isn't marching.'

'Turn it up,' growled Mr Farlow. 'What's going on in this car? Why all the backbiting?'

Jillian looked downright miserable and Ray blushed.

'What are you doing afterwards, Mick?' Ray said, to cover up.

'Going home, I s'pose.'

37

'We're going to the football. Dad's driving us up to the city. Then we're having dinner in a restaurant.'

Mr Farlow's forefinger started tapping the wheel and Michael sneezed until he rattled, trying to smother his face in his sleeve and yearning for the open air.

'We'd ask you if we could, of course,' Mrs Farlow said, 'but we're picking up others farther on.'

'Are we?' squeaked Ray. 'I thought we were having the day on our own.'

'No, dear. You couldn't have forgotten. The Morgans.'

'*All* of them?'

'No, dear, of course not.'

'Who then? Not blooming Iris and Vera? I couldn't stand them.'

'No, dear. Not the girls.'

'Who then?'

Even Jillian, who was bottom of the class in everything, was beginning to look uncomfortable and Mr Farlow snapped more sharply than he intended, 'Michael, I'll drop you at the War Memorial. I think you'd better wait there for the march.'

'That he will,' said Mrs Farlow, 'make no mistake. It's a dreadful cold you've got, Michael. Sneezing your germs all over the place. I can't understand your grandmother. What did she let you out for, dressed for midsummer? Don't you go into the hall for lemonade or anything, mixing with other people. I think you've sneezed enough damage for one morning. You go straight home as soon as the march is over.'

He was out on the pavement, trying to catch his breath, with the smell of seaweed as sharp as a knife in his nostrils.

'Yes, Mrs Farlow.'

'And make sure you stand under cover.'

'Yes, Mrs Farlow.'

'Then home, and into bed.'

38

'Yes, Mrs Farlow.'

'See you, Mick,' said Ray.

'Yes, Mrs Farlow.'

The car door slammed, expelling a blast of musky air into his face, a final indignity that produced a shattering convulsion of sneezes.

Jillian looked back as they drew away but couldn't see him. A crowd was there and rain streaked the rear window. She was hurt and bewildered, wondering why such an awful wall stood between them. Mum had put it there simply because she had peeped through a fence. It was not her fault he hadn't had his clothes on. It was not his fault either. Each had been as surprised as the other.

'Blooming Mick,' Ray complained. 'What a nut! What's wrong with him?'

Mr Farlow growled, 'Enough! I'm shocked. What are you people trying to do to that boy? He's a nice kid. I wouldn't be ashamed to own him.'

Mrs Farlow folded her hands in her lap and looked angry.

Her husband frowned. 'I ought to call in on the Morgans and fill the car up with them! That'd be justice.'

CHAPTER FOUR

The street was full of parked cars and people, of shop verandas dripping into gutters, of trees drooping in wet air, and Michael groped away from them, trying to find privacy. Trees and shops and people were of peculiar form, like pictures with bleared lines and overrunning colours, dissolving. His eyes streamed and his nostrils burned and his face was a horrible mess that he longed to thrust into a bowl of water or mop with a towel. Everywhere he turned he seemed to be confronted by people who were staring at him as if they enjoyed his discomfort. 'Rotten lot,' he groaned and closed his hands over his face, dragging at his eyes with his fingertips, trying to clear his vision, not knowing what to do or where to go or how to re-establish his dignity.

'Hey, young Mick!'

It was Bully Boy MacBaren, seen indistinctly, with hair as red as a light for danger. Bully Boy, maybe with a grin, and with Warren Flack tagging at his elbow—Flackie, they called him, the kid who lived behind the fruiterer's shop and smelt faintly of decaying cabbages.

'Got a fly in your eye, young Mick? Here, lemme help.'

'Yeh, Mick, let us help.' Flackie was always like an echo, tagging along in the shadow of someone bigger.

Michael backed away from them, shivering, hating the Farlows for everything, and Grandma for not waking up when she should have, and the men in his family for never being near him when he wanted them. He was always on his own with the world against him.

'Hey. Look out, young Mick.'

But he had backed too far and stumbled against the bluestone kerb round the War Memorial. He threw out his hands to save himself, and sprawled, exposing his face.

Bully Boy grinned at him. 'Why don't you wipe it on your shirt, Mick. . . .?'

But he heard no more. He ran, blazing with shame, off through the dark cypress-trees in the grove where the War Memorial stood, down the straight tea-tree lane through the foreshore, and on to the beach down onto the wet desert of sand where nothing moved except a brown dog, burrowing. He looked back in fear, certain of pursuit, but no one was there, and he folded into a heap and wept, trying to wipe his eyes on his sleeve but having to drag out his shirt tails to mop everything up, to blow his nose repeatedly, to surrender completely to his shame.

It wasn't fair. The rain still dribbled over him, not warmly any more, and he couldn't stop shivering from nerves. How could such a morning have gone so wrong?

It was Anzac Day. He had wanted to be one of the crowd. He had wanted to stir to the music of the Salvation Army Band. It didn't matter what Dad said about glorifying force; it was terrific stirring to the band, feeling strong enough to punch someone in the eye. He had wanted to walk along the footpath to the rhythm of the band, perhaps matching his stride for a few modest moments to the strides of the men who had fought in the wars. Other kids could do it out in the open with their dads; he had to sneak it in quietly behind the crowd; not overdoing it, because he was big now. No one would have minded. They'd only have smiled in a kind way. But he was on his own again and nothing was there except, vaguely, a greasy sea, more green than blue, more grey than green, and a brown dog in the sand, that brown dog kneeling like a little girl in the sand, watching him open-mouthed, with a frown.

He rubbed hard at his eyes.

It was true. It was a girl.

'Oh, crikey,' he groaned and wanted to run again, wanted to get away somewhere to live it down. She had watched him all the time, must have heard him cry, must have seen his face before he mopped it dry. 'Oh, *crikey*. . . .' He could have cried all over again.

'Hullo,' she said. 'Are you sick?'

He didn't want to talk to her. He hated her, just for being there. She *made* him sick, just by being there.

'What are you snivelling for?' she said. 'Are you a cry-baby or something?'

He compressed his lips with irritation and turned his head away, and with painful self-consciousness pushed himself to his feet and tried to stuff his shirt back into his shorts, shaking all over.

She, too, stood up and brushed the sand from her hands and knees and edged closer on tiptoe, with uncertainty, like someone curious to confirm whether an object seen was harmless or dangerous. 'What's your name?' she said. 'I'm Margaret.'

He still had no word for her. He wanted only to vanish into the earth, but was intrigued, against his wish, by her ridiculous stance, stuck up on tiptoe, long neck craned, as if she might pounce like a cat or suddenly take flight into the distance. But he was very cross with her. It had been a dog on the sand, not a rain-soaked little girl dressed in brown. Something called Lady or Rover, not Margaret. Something that barked maybe, certainly not something that stood up on its hind legs and started talking.

'Your Mum won't be pleased with you,' she said, 'blowing your nose on your shirt.'

He was getting frantic with his shirt, trying to poke

42

it out of sight. The stupid thing still hung out in odd places like a badge of shame and *wouldn't* go back where it should have been. His shorts were too tight at the waist.

'Don't you speak English?' she said. 'Are you French or Italian or something? My Mum says I started speaking English when I was nine months old. I just upped and started, she says.'

'It was a dog,' he exploded indignantly. 'It was a dog down there.'

'What was a dog?' She glanced behind her with anxiety.

'You were,' he wailed, pushing at the horrible shirt.

She shook her head solemnly. 'Oh no, I've never been a dog. I was an angel in the Christmas play and the dormouse in Alice. I was the princess in Sleeping Beauty and Donny Clayton got into trouble with Miss Lang because he kissed me like he shouldn't ought to.' She giggled. 'My name's Margaret. What's yours?'

The idiotic shirt; how could any shirt get into such a tangle? And wiping tears on it and blowing his nose all over it while *she* was looking.

'I'll tuck it in for you.'

'You will not.'

'I tuck Norman's in after he's been to the lavatory.'

'Well, I'm not Norman.'

'Norman's my little brother.'

'That's his bad luck.'

But she got at him somehow, even though his eyes almost popped and he did his best to avoid her. She got a tenacious hold on his shirt and started pushing it into his pants. 'Hey,' he yelled, 'hey, ease up. What the heck do you think you're doing?' He broke away from her violently, outraged. 'You take your hands off me, you little twirp. You keep your hands to yourself. I'm a boy.'

She looked astonished. 'I hope so. My word I do. Because you don't behave like a lady.'

He stood with hands on hips, head jerking from side to side, his defences in disarray. 'You leave my pants alone,' he wailed. 'You go somewhere else. I don't care what you do to your brother; you can't do it to me. I'm a big boy. You don't even know me.'

'Well, that's not my fault. You haven't told me your name. I've told you who I am. I'm Margaret.'

'Yeh, yeh, I know. I must have heard a dozen times.' He didn't know how to handle her, had never met anything like it, and without realizing it had unbuttoned the waist-band of his shorts and was angrily tidying his shirt.

'Go on,' she urged, 'tell me.'

Her voice had a wheedling tone, a teasing tone, that was awfully grown-up and sure of itself.

'It's *Michael*,' he admitted explosively and was immediately mad with her for getting it out of him and even madder with himself for revealing it. There had been a certain safety in keeping that vital information to himself. She couldn't talk about him if she didn't know his name, couldn't tell anyone she had seen him blubbing his eyes out, all covered in goo, blowing his nose on his shirt. Now *everyone* would know.

'Do you bite your fingernails, too?' she said, almost reading his mind.

'No!' He glared at her defiantly.

'Phil does. Phil's my big brother. Mum's always nagging him about it. They look *gruesome*. Do you always blow your nose on your shirt?'

'Of course I don't. I've never done it before. Ever.'

'I'm not allowed to blow my nose on my dress.'

He breathed out noisily and impatiently. 'I don't suppose you are. Anyway, I wasn't blowing my nose, no matter what you thought. It was Mrs Farlow's rotten old perfume. Rotten old stuff. I reckon she must have bought it at the zoo.' The injustice of the whole thing

44

was throbbing like a sore thumb and that he should be bothering, inexplicably, to defend himself for her benefit made it so much worse. He didn't want to be bothered with her. 'You shouldn't have been looking,' he grumbled. 'It wasn't fair of you to look. It was *private*. Anyway, you were a dog.'

'I wasn't a dog.'

'You *were*.'

She tossed her head, and her hair, a stringy colour, flapped in wet strands. 'You ought to wear glasses then,' she said, "cos I was a cat. Do you want to hear me meow?'

'No!'

She mewed so realistically that his eyes, despite himself, had to dart to left and right to make sure that a cat was not around. 'I can't bark, though. Boys bark. I'm not a boy. I'm nine and a half. My birthday's October the third. How old are you?'

But that he would not tell her. That, he refused to say. He was not going to be pushed around by a kid of nine, or knocked half-senseless with her chatter. Yet out it came. 'Thirteen.' Loud and clear with a defensive ring to it.

'Ooh,' she said. 'You're little for thirteen.'

'I'm *what*?' he yelled. 'I'm not little for thirteen.' He stood up straight, incensed and insulted, arms folded across his chest like a man. 'I'm taller than lots of kids of thirteen.'

'But I bet you're littler than all the rest.'

He looked at her warily, not sure whether her words made sense or not. He repeated them in his head and there was sense in them all right. She was sharp for a little kid of nine. 'That's a silly sort of argument,' he grumbled.

She giggled, confirming in him the fear that, in some horrible female way that had nothing to do with age, she was making a monkey out of him. What with Grandma and Mrs Farlow and crummy Jillian and *her* he had had enough of females for one day. Little creep she was.

'Do you live here?' she said.

'What,' he sneered, 'on the beach?'

She regarded him blandly, so patiently, and with such condescension that his brief feeling of superiority collapsed like a bubble. 'Michael,' she sighed, 'I don't mean that.'

He grimaced. 'Of course I live here. Where else would I live if I'm hanging around the beach at this hour of the morning? But I'm not telling you where, see!'

She shrugged her small shoulders. 'It doesn't matter to me where you live. I don't care. I'm a witch. I just fly around. I give my magic ring a twist and go anywhere I please. If I want to go to your house I just give it a twist and off I go. Have you got a magic ring?'

Michael groaned and closed his eyes and turned his mouth into a thin line, just as Dad had a habit of doing when he had taken about all that flesh and blood could stand.

'Yesterday I was in Africa,' she said brightly. 'Tomorrow I think I'll go to Tasmania. Why don't you buy a magic ring? We witches don't use brooms any more. I got mine from Mrs Dwyer. It cost six cents with a stick of chewing gum. Isn't it lovely?' She extended her right forefinger. The ring was a gold colour with a chip of red glass set in it to look like a ruby. 'Magic,' she said, gravely shaking her head, and almost went to turn it through the magic circle but suddenly drew her left hand away quickly. 'Ooh, careless,' she whispered, 'must never twist it. Never without wishing for something first or anything might happen.' She looked up at a sharp angle, huge eyes wide with white. Something about the shape of her face, or her expression, or just her, troubled him.

46

'I might disappear,' she said. 'Pooffff. Into nothing. The chewing-gum's good, too. You can blow big bubbles with it. They go *pop*. I told my Mum I got it in a packet of fizzy stuff because she says that well-bred ladies don't chew gum. I'll bet Queen Elizabeth chews gum though, don't you?'

He knew that the band had struck up at the other end of town. The thud of the base drum was beating in his feet. He wanted to be there, so much to be there. Maybe he could sneak in at the back, hang around at the edges. Bully Boy wouldn't see.

'I'll bet Queen Elizabeth does just anything she pleases. One day I'll give my magic ring a special twist and be Queen for a whole day and send all the children home from school. Then Queen Elizabeth can be me and do my piano practice.'

'Yeh,' he said, 'yeh, you do that.' The beat of the band was beating into him with insistence. Bully Boy wouldn't start anything with a crowd around. He should have thought of that before, but of course he couldn't have pulled his shirt out at the foot of the War Memorial.

'Do you think I should?'

'Yeh, yeh. Terrific.'

'Should I do it now?'

'Should you do what?'

'Twist my ring and be Queen Elizabeth and give all the children a holiday.'

'That'd be silly, wouldn't it?' He was trying to get away.

'Why would it be silly?'

'Because it *is* a holiday.'

'What is?'

'Today! Anzac Day! You can hear the band, can't you? You can hear them coming.'

'I'm not silly, Michael. I'm not talking about today.

47

I'm talking about next Monday. You don't listen, do you?'

'You didn't say anything about Monday!'

'I did too.'

'You're a bloomin' little liar. You didn't say any such thing.'

Her eyes opened wide and her lips became a puckered-up circle. 'Ooooh,' she said, 'you *swore* at me.'

'I bally well didn't!' He was yelling again.

'You won't go to Heaven if you swear. You mustn't *ever* swear at girls.'

'Aw, come off it. You're a proper ratbag.'

'Phil wouldn't talk to me like that. Phil wouldn't be allowed. Your sister wouldn't be very pleased if she knew.'

'I haven't got a sister and I don't think I'd want one, either. I reckon not having a sister is about the only good thing that's ever happened to me. You go and twist your ring somewhere. Turn yourself into a block of flats or something. I'm going to the march; *goodbye*.'

He took about four paces along the beach, with his head spinning, and her piping voice came after him. 'You should have a sister, Michael. Then you might be polite. You should ask your Mum to buy one.'

He turned on her, completely exasperated. 'Buy one? Strike me, you don't *buy* babies. You get 'em for nothing. Anyway, I haven't got a Mum.'

'Did your Mum go away?' She looked very grave, very concerned.

'No, she didn't.'

'Did your Mum die?'

To his intense embarrassment a lump in his throat almost choked off his voice. 'Yes. . . .'

'My Granny's dead,' she said. 'So's my Uncle Matt. But he drank. My guinea pig, too.'

He swallowed. 'Your guinea pig *drank*?'

'My guinea pig's dead.'

His insides felt as though a little man had got in there somehow and was stirring with a spoon. She was worse than Jillian. Jillian was only dumb. This one was a raving lunatic.

'You don't like guinea pigs, do you? I can see it on your face. I think they're beautiful. I was sad when my guinea pig died. Our cat killed a bird. I was sad that day, too. But I wasn't the cat. When I'm a cat I'm kind to birds.'

His complaint welled up and poured out. 'I'm going to the march. I'm going to the march. I bally well am. I'm not going to stand here listening to you. That beaut band——'

'The *band*,' she said. 'That silly old band.' She pulled a long face. 'You ought to hear my Mum talk about bands.'

'Don't you call it silly. It's terrific. Those fellows come down every year, all the way from town, and don't charge a penny. I know. My Grandma tells me. All they get is something to eat and then they go home.'

'Boom, boom. Bang, bang. Squeak, squawk, squobble.'

Michael was shocked. 'Don't you talk that way about the Salvos. I know all about them. Even my Dad reckons the Salvos are worth their salt. They help in all the wars. They help poor people. They do all sorts of things you'd never know about.'

She put her finger to her lips and rolled her eyes and looked about six years of age, as if he should have been caring for her instead of yelling at her. Nothing like her had ever happened to him. He still didn't know what to do with her, shuddered all over, shook with temper.

'Goodness me,' she said, 'you're funny.'

It was like trying to get through to a different sort of creature that didn't think like a human. Yet he

49

couldn't get away from her. She seemed to hold him in a spell. But that band was coming down Main Street and he wasn't there to see it. All the men were marching. All the kids were marching. They'd all be in step, swinging along.

'Aw, crikey,' he wailed. 'Look, Margaret; I want to go.'

'I'm not stopping you.'

Which was perfectly true. She wasn't. But he seemed stuck.

'I'm going,' he said.

'Go. I don't care. Phil never wants to play with me either.'

'Look,' he said, 'you shouldn't be here. You come with me. It's not right for little girls to be on their own. It's dangerous.'

'What's dangerous?'

'Being on your own!'

'Why? I'm not going to hit myself, am I?'

He made a whimpering sound. 'Because! That's why!'

'But I'm not on my own. You're here. I think you're silly or something.'

'That's what I'm saying.' He banged his fist into his side. 'When I go I won't be.'

'Oh,' she said, then looked up brightly. 'Won't be what?'

He spun on his toes in complete bewilderment, almost losing his balance. 'What are you doing here, anyway?' he yelped. 'You're drenched. What are you doing out in the rain?'

'Getting wet,' she said, 'same as you.'

'I'm not wet!'

'You are too. Sniffling all the time. Have you got a weak chest or something? Mum always hangs a piece of camphor in a little bag round my neck in winter. Mum says all the Hamworths have had bags of camphor round their necks for hundreds of years.'

50

He groaned.

'You ought to tell your Dad you want a bag of camphor like the Hamworths have.'

'Bust the blooming Hamworths!'

'The Hamworths *never* get colds.'

'Nor do I,' he exploded. 'I'm sniffing because I can't blow my nose.'

'Why don't you blow it like the men on the road do? You know. Stick a finger up it and snort.'

His face twisted with disgust. 'You *horrible* little girl.'

She turned coy again. 'You could use your shirt. Go on, Michael, pull your shirt out. I won't tell.'

'I wish you'd go away somewhere,' he said, his voice climbing higher. 'I do. I wish you'd twist that stupid old ring of yours. Why don't you give it a twist and fly away?'

'I don't want to. That's why.'

'Because you *can't*, you mean. Because your ring's not magic at all. Because you're just a silly little girl making up stories.'

Her eyes widened to huge circles. 'You don't believe in magic rings?' she squealed. 'You think I'm making it all up?'

'Of course you're making it up.'

'You think I'm a fibber or something?'

'I don't think, I know. You'd be the champion of the world, I reckon.'

'And I was a cat when you came down to the beach and you still think I'm fibbing?'

'You were a *dog*,' he bellowed.

'I was a cat!'

'You were a *dog*. I saw you. I should know.'

CHAPTER FIVE

Dad was leading the march. How could he be out in full public view, looking sure of himself, looking marvellous, as though nothing in the world mattered except getting from one end of Main Street to the other in a dead straight line? No one would guess from Dad that there'd been a thundering row. They'd got out of the car and Dad had started shaking his mates by the hand, beaming left, right and centre, chatting to them, slapping them on the shoulders; it was a change of mood so fast it was breathtaking. Ray knew what the red flush round his neck meant, but no one else noticed. Maybe Jillian knew, but not Mum. Mum was much too upset, and still looked it, to notice anything. 'That boy brings us nothing but trouble,' she had finished on a shrill note. 'I cannot understand why you defend him.'

Dad's control was fantastic. One moment yelling, 'If you don't shut up I'll be driving up a tree.' The next moment out of the car, smiling, 'Nice to see you, Archdeacon. Glad you could make it.'

Marching along with the Scouts with Dad out in front was a special feeling. It made Ray a bit shy, more than usually conscious of himself, and he felt that people following at the roadside were saying, 'That's Jack Farlow's son. Chip off the old block, isn't he?' But he wasn't. He might have the look of Dad about him, but it was skin deep. Dad took everything in his stride, but when Ray got embarrassed or upset his feet felt as big as dinner plates and he was almost scared to put them down.

52

Everything had been warm and special until Mick had blundered in. Blooming Mick Cameron. Mum and Dad at each other's throats. Every time Mick Cameron crossed their paths there was a row. Give him ten seconds and he could wreck anything. Couldn't sit quietly in the car like anyone else but had to sneeze and shudder and gasp and put on a terrible act. Dad should have had the brains not to go back, Mum had told him not to, because when Mick Cameron was around everything went taut and you didn't get over it in a couple of minutes. Never, probably. Mick Cameron had done his dash long ago. It kept nagging at you, kept taking the edge off everything. Turning even Dad's big morning sour.

Dad was a huge man and by sticking his head a bit out of line and by raising himself to his toes Ray could glimpse his bare head way out in front in the rain, as square as a block of stone above the crowd, Dad's head between two wet flags. He had boomed, '*Parade. By the left. Quick march!*' And the drummer had crashed on the base drum as if he had thought with Dad's mind, and everyone had stepped out, all the kids and women and men. Even fellows who had been colonels and wing-commanders stepped out to Dad's command.

Dad with a machine-gun all those years and years ago. Dad only twenty-one, leaping into that hole on his own as if he didn't care whether he lived or died. How could you believe it of him? Dad, so kind and gentle, leaping into that hole with a blood-curdling bellow. 'How'd you do it, Dad? I can't understand it. They could have shot you dead. You could have lain dead in the jungle, sinking into the mud, and I'd never have been born. There'd have been no Jillian. There'd have been nothing of us Farlows. Did you care, Dad? Did you know you were risking our lives too? Don't you ever wake up at nights, worrying, having to kill thirteen blokes so we could be born?'

53

'There were bullies in the world,' Dad said, 'and the bully is no friend of mine. The odds were thirteen to one. I'm not ashamed.'

Dad way out there in front looked proud.

'They're coming,' Flackie said, with an itch in his feet to join the crowd.

But Bruce MacBaren shrugged.

'Come on, let's go,' Flackie wanted to say, but didn't, because no one, particularly Warren Flack, told Bruce what to do.

Sticking close to Bruce was to feel like somebody, and feeling like that made up for other things. It had been good seeing that toffee-nosed Cameron kid take off like a rabbit. That was what being close to Bruce meant; you got respect.

'Hi, Bruce. Hi, Flackie,' kids would say, trying to sound matey, but you knew they were shaking like jellies. It made you feel good, feel safe, feel tough, like you were six feet tall when Bruce was standing there.

He almost had to pinch himself sometimes to make sure it was real. Bruce MacBaren, Warren Flack's mate for seven weeks. 'Hi, kid,' he had said that day, 'how are you doing?' And it hadn't been a threat. It was like coming in out of a storm that had lasted all his life. Warren had always been on the outer, like a stray dog, always getting pushed. Being nice got him nowhere, trying hard at school got him nowhere because he never got anything right unless he copied it or had a book open on the seat. And being himself, seventh kid in a family of nine, just trying to get his share, was like being lost. Other kids in big families seemed to have a whale of a time, but Ma was worn into the ground and Pop worked twelve hours a day in his shop. But now he was Bruce MacBaren's mate.

Bruce standing there, leaning against a tree in a

mannish way, licking with the tip of his tongue at the corner of his mouth, both hands thrust into the pockets of his raincoat; Flackie himself standing the same way, except for the tree, swaying a bit on his heels to look tough. Bruce said he didn't care about the march; marching along to the Salvo's beat was for little kids and old men. Bruce was there to stake his claim on lemonade and cakes. But the itch was in Flackie's feet and the drum-beat was in his blood. They were coming down his street and coming fast, because Main Street was short. Not long, the way it used to be as he remembered it first —a trek to school and a frantic run to get across. He had been born on Main Street, had lived a life on it. The cops had said to Ma, 'Keep that boy off the street.' She had shrugged. 'Do I chain him up? Do I say go play in a banana case? Have you got nine kids, Mister, in a twenty-by-thirty yard full of crates?'

'What's eatin' you, Flackie?' Bruce said. 'Do you wish you were marching with the kids?'

'Yeh. Like I wish for a hole in the head.'

They were coming down his street, the crowd pressing round the parked cars, little kids pacing it out along the footpaths swinging their arms, flags and banners swaying out in the centre and the Salvos coming with cheeks as red as apples, thudding on the drums, trombones and trumpets gleaming in the wet, and Bruce MacBaren's tongue licking at his lips *in marching time*.

All the men swinging along, Ray could *feel* it now, men who looked tired and haggard every other day of the week, squaring their shoulders and taking off their hats to let the rain spatter in their hair, swinging along as if they were young again, even old drunk Harry out of gaol by a freak swinging along without a limp. All the Guides and Brownies and Scouts and Cubs swinging along, grinning at each other, snared in the beat, arms swinging shoulder high, feeling like princesses and kings. They got teased sometimes for doing good deeds and thinking pure thoughts and all that stuff, but not when they were swinging along with the men and real medals jingled to the beat. Dad out in front looking fantastic. Mum swinging along with the nurses and aides, looking more like herself now; Jillian swinging along even cracking a smile.

Mick Cameron was a flea. Who cared about Mick? He could jump in the lake.

CHAPTER SIX

Michael seemed to be looking at himself again; from a distance he seemed to be regarding the view with astonishment. There he stood with hands on hips, red in the face from exasperation, sniffing like mad, arguing on a deserted beach with a little squirt of a girl about whether she was a cat or a dog.

'Ar, baloney,' he bellowed. 'What are you trying to do to me? Turn me into a nut? You weren't a cat and you weren't a dog. My eyes were all runny; I was sneezing my head off; I couldn't see a foot in front of my face.'

She sighed, jerking her shoulders. 'Mum calls me Tiddles when I'm a cat, so if you're not nice to me I'll turn back into a cat and spit. I've got sharp claws, too. I'm a tortoiseshell cat.'

He turned away from her, discovering entirely to his surprise that he *could* turn away from her, and more, that he could *walk* away from her.

'You're not going to dare me, are you?' she cried, calling after him. 'You wouldn't have me turn back into a cat in front of your very eyes.'

'I haven't got eyes in the middle of me back!'

'You'd die. That's what'd happen to you. You'd die stone dead of fright if I turned into a cat. I turned into a rat once and Mrs Hershell screamed and screamed and screamed.'

He broke into a run, floundering off through the soft sand. 'You're silly,' he yelled into the air. 'Turn into a cat if you want to, I don't care.' But he was running along the beach and had not meant to do that. He had intended to go back to the road, but she had him in a muddle. 'You're stupid,' he yelled over his shoulder and ploughed off into the tea-tree, stubbornly looking ahead, refusing to look back. He got a good distance into the tea-tree and there stopped to find his breath, but at once felt the thud of drums again and the sound of brass and the presence of people moving as a body—so close their approach could have been through the tea-tree, marching into it; so close that in a moment they must march over the top of him, on into the sea. They'd sink beneath the waves singing about God our help in ages past and sons flying forgotten as a dream.

'You little horror,' he shouted fiercely. 'You've made me miss the march.'

He dragged his shirt out, blew his nose with angry snorts, and broke through to the lane. A whistle-blast sounded and the band stopped.

'There,' he yelled furiously. 'I told you so. You little creep.'

His voice was appallingly loud, like a bomb-burst in church. He gasped, and all the people up by the War Memorial in the cypress grove turned their heads and looked. Straight down the tea-tree lane they glared as if they had searchlights in their heads. He tried to shrink but felt bigger than a house, felt like a great tall building with Michael Cameron's head on top.

Glared and stared. Like nailing him to a wall with spears of ice. Bully Boy, too. Bully Boy was there with that head like a light for danger, holding up an arm with a fist on the end of it. Waving maybe, threatening maybe; perhaps saying, 'Yeh, that's him. Who else? The Cameron kid.'

Now everyone would know who was acting the clown and Mrs Farlow would know because she knew everything and Grandma would get to hear of it. Of course! It was enough to make a fellow sick.

Oh, to be like silly Margaret. To possess a ring that one could twist to vanish in a puff of smoke. He slunk into the tea-tree and the eyes followed him like searchlights glaring on his back, grown-ups' eyes and Bully Boy's eyes and the blooming Farlows' no doubt. 'Just like a Cameron,' Mrs F. would be saying. 'All tarred with the same brush. No respect for the feelings of other people.' Which just wasn't true.

Not a foot could he put right. And he had wanted to stand quietly in the crowd and think about Mum. 'Golly, Mum,' he said. 'Can't you stick your bib in? Can't you do something for a fellow? Like striking everyone dead?'

He stamped his foot, stamped on a tree root, and jarred himself to the nape of his neck, tears starting from his eyes. The whole surface of the earth to stamp on and his heel had to crack down on wood as hard as rock. He shivered with rage and groaned against the tree and gave the splayed trunk a vicious backhander to square the account, then held the poor hand limply aloft expecting his fingers to drop off. 'Holy cow,' he whimpered, 'I'm barmy. I'm a nut.' And slid and sat and huddled, so stunned by hurts that he didn't know what hurt most. Some fellows were born lucky and some were born smart, but Mick Cameron had been chucked into the world on a day when nothing good had been left lying around to pick up; they'd cut him loose, smacked his bottom, and chucked him out, tumbling him down to earth through space, over and over, arms and legs flapping like old rope. Crunch. He had hit rock and not got over the shock. 'The world,' Dad said, 'is gas, liquid and rock.'

Michael moaned. 'Just for once, couldn't *I* be right?' Throbbing all over, not even seeing straight, a hole in his stomach as if it had been gouged out with a knife. 'I'm sick to bloomin' death of being everybody's joke.

I'll show 'em I'm no joke. I'll stab 'em or shoot 'em or something. I'll kill 'em. I'll show 'em the earth's made of rock—I'll hit 'em on the head with it. I'll *spatter* 'em.' But he limped off through the gloomy trees again to the beach.

It was open there and silent and safe.

Margaret had gone.

He stood, but drooped, limp of body and limp of heart, as if his vitals were bleeding into the sand.

It was awfully quiet back at the War Memorial. Were they laying their wreaths on the ground?

Margaret had gone. Got him into all that trouble and then run.

He wouldn't admit it, wouldn't make a thought of it, but knew it just the same: he was sorry. He was sad she wasn't there. Horrid little girl, stupid little thing. Then he saw her some distance away down by the water. 'Huh,' he grumbled. 'Look at her. Couldn't pick her from a dog. Same as before. Cat, my eye.'

He looked the other way, suddenly feeling his hurts again and objecting to the curious longing for her company. But the beach was empty for miles and the sea was grey. He glanced back and frowned.

'She's stupid. Making out like a dog. Sniffing around the sand. If a wave comes in it'll break all over her. . . . Hey!' he shouted. 'Serve you right if you get dunked!'

Then he remembered the glaring grown-ups, remembered them uneasily like an evil he had done, and fell silent with guilt. 'I'll kill 'em. . . .'

She was awfully like a dog. There wasn't any argument. He sighed and shuffled off down the sand towards her, wanting to go but not wanting to go, and with his hand still throbbing as if he had hit it with an axe, his heel feeling bruised and the pit of his stomach feeling sick.

It *was* a dog.

He stopped in the middle of a shuffling stride and

glanced both ways and without knowing it curled a forefinger around his chin, and pulled at his chin, pinching it, plucking at it.

It wasn't a dog of course. It was a trick of the light. He had been sneezing too much. Maybe she was right. Maybe he ought to wear glasses. Maybe he'd upset his optic nerves or something hammering his foot against the root.

He took another step and stopped again, feeling peculiar to a slight degree. It wasn't a trick of the light. She had four legs and a tail.

'Ar—phooey!'

There weren't any witches! Not of that kind! Present-day witches, Dad said, were people who liked to dance in circles without any clothes, Dad giving him a bit of a glare at the time, as if reckoning that Mick had better watch his step. This four-legged creature was an innocent little dog, with as much to do with Margaret as a clockwork mouse.

'Anyway, you don't call dogs *Tiddles*. . . . Hey! Margaret! If you're a cat I'm a canary. Do you want to hear me tweet?'

He sneered and walked away a half-dozen or so paces, his heart beating harder than he felt it should have done; but when he looked back the dog was giving him the eye, with one ear lying flat and the other ear cocked. Impishly? With that stupid round-eyed look she had worn herself? It was Mrs Ellis's mongrel terrier! Sure it was. Except that Mrs Ellis's terrier should have had a large white spot.

'Once upon a time . . .' Grandma occasionally said, forgetting he was grown-up. That was where witches belonged: in bedside stories that scared you stiff when you were six. When you were thirteen, witches were wet.

Again he seemed to stand off at a distance and look at himself. Standing off like that, looking back, he wanted to deride himself, wanted to scoff, 'Mick Cameron, you're a twit.' But he wasn't standing off, he was there on the spot, reluctantly transfixed, asking questions of himself, *scientifically*, using Dad's technique.

'Is she on the beach? Can you see her anywhere? Did she pass you in the lane? Did she head out to sea for a dip? Is she a nut? Did she go on up to the War Memorial? She didn't, you bally well know that, so what's she done with herself? Have you seen her before? Ever? You know by sight every kid in the place, but this one you've never clapped eyes on in your life. Is that stupid bit of tin magic like she says? Power of the mind and all that stuff. Is she a horrible old hag with warts on her beak and hair like *string*?'

He laughed aloud, jeering at himself, and scooped up a handful of sand and threw it with all his might and the dog was off in an instant, stubby tail down, ears flat. 'Garn,' he yelled after it, 'now turn into a girl. I'll bet you couldn't to save your life.' But the dog ran off and the beach was empty again, quite empty, and up at the War Memorial they were singing a mournful hymn, as if they were crying in tune with lumps in their throats.

'Michael!' That shrill, piping voice!

His heart bumped, but she was not about, not in sight. She must have been lying low somewhere, teasing him, probably giggling to herself because he had been talking to a dog as if he had hoped for the dog to talk back. He felt so mixed up, so uncertain of himself, and kicked at the sand and suddenly sat cross-legged not many paces from the quietly lapping sea, sat there and brooded and scowled.

It was a huge world of water unmarked except faintly by the funnel of a ship out where visibility ended. Metal out there on the horizon, mined from the rock, melted, cooled, beaten into shape, welded with blue flame and spitting sparks. It was a ship with a throbbing engine built by men. A ship was lucky to be a ship; it knew what it was.

It was all right for those grown-up Clever Dicks with their gases and liquids and rock being rock. Being a boy was different from that. Maybe they'd never been boys at all, Dad or Richard or Gregory. Maybe they'd been born six feet tall with size ten boots on, with answers to everything learnt off pat. Never for them having to wonder about the things that grandmothers said. *They* didn't listen, just shut their ears or shook their heads or went away smiling. Things like stupid little girls didn't worry them. Things like sad people or happy people or stories or songs or Salvation Army bands or kids with heads full of crazy imaginings didn't matter to them unless they could add them up like sums. Two and two made four in *their* world. Wouldn't it have been great for once if they made three or ninety-eight or a thousand and one and he was the fellow to prove it? 'What?' they'd have gasped. 'Two and two can't make ninety-eight!' And their eyes would have stood out on stalks and their pants would have dropped from shock.

The ship wasn't there any more but loping waves were beginning to come in, rolling in from a mile away where the invisible ship thrust on, and he had to shuffle back or get soaked. He bared his teeth at it. No ship to see but its stupid waves were rolling in. The ordinary, dreary, matter-of-fact cause always had to be right. You couldn't get waves without something ordinary to stir them up. Rock was rock.

It would be terrific meeting a real live witch who could turn into a frog with a pop. It would be terrific striking the sea to send it rolling back. It would be terrific having a magic lamp with a genie in it. 'Hail, Master. Shall we thrash Bully Boy to a pulp or fly to the moon or turn that horrible school into a slice of cheese and eat it for lunch?'

'That rotten Margaret. Of course I didn't think her up. She made too much noise to be thought up out of anything. But people don't turn into dogs, specially when they reckon they're cats.'

His scowl darkened. 'Six cents and a stick of chewing-gum. Does she think anyone's going to believe that?'

He drew irritable wriggles in the sand.

'Well, this fellow's not going to believe it, no sir. Dad's right. So's Richard. Grandma's got bats in the belfry. The bloomin' dog was on the beach all the time. She can turn into a horse in front of my very eyes and I still won't believe it. She can flap around like a bird and I still won't believe it.'

He sneezed.

'And I wouldn't wear a bag with camphor in it round my neck to save my life. What's *camphor*, anyway? Something they mix up out of bat's blood and toads? I bet it stinks worse than Mrs Farlow's perfume.'

He sneaked a glance along the beach again, both ways: no Margaret, no dog, no cat. He was as alone as a shag on a rock and those people were still singing that hymn, that horrible mournful hymn. It must have had a thousand verses. All those people up there out of sight, that whopping great crowd, and he was alone; that crowd with a hole in the middle of it marked Michael, exactly where he should have been standing. Everybody gathered round the War Memorial looking sad, dabbing at their eyes, sniffing, not even the kids glancing round to ask why Michael Cameron was missing. Everyone knew him but no one cared.

'I thought you were going to the Anzac thing.'

His heart bumped.

It was her; silly Margaret.

'I've been a cat again,' she said, and mewed.

He wouldn't look at her, wouldn't give her that satisfaction, because if she were not a girl he knew

64

perfectly well she *had* to be a dog, and a talking dog was more than he wished to face.

'I wasn't a tortoiseshell cat, though. I was a teeny-weeny tabby.'

His mouth twisted but his heart thumped like mad and he could feel her presence though nothing of her touched him. Her legs stretched out on the wet sand, ordinary legs with laced-up shoes, but the rest of her he would not look at.

'I heard you sneeze again,' she said. 'Sneezes break the spell. You ought to be more careful with your sneezing. So I came right down out of the tree and the dog got an awful fright and ran away. You'll have to go to bed to get better.'

Imagine it? *Wanting* her to come back? He must have been crazy.

'I've never been a tabby before. That must have been your fault. You're lucky the fright didn't kill me. Turning into a *tabby*! Dogs chase tabbies but they're scared of tortoiseshell cats. That dog chased me, it did —all along the beach and up a tree, and I called and called and you didn't come. I think you're a meanie.'

Michael sighed, almost tiredly. 'I think you're barmy.' Then found himself waiting for the continuing chatter that didn't come. Instead, he felt her go silent, felt a difference, and realized the difference had been there from the moment she had come back. Her voice had not charged along as it had done before. He glanced at her and the difference was in her face, faintly a look of hurt. It surprised him and something in him turned hard.

'You were hiding,' he drawled.

'I was not.'

'I bet you were,' and suddenly he knew that by not shouting at her he might get the better of her. When he shouted it was a game. He was thirteen; she was only a little kid; it was his right to be the boss.

'How could you get a magic ring for six cents? It'd cost thousands of dollars. You'd have to go to Arabia or somewhere to buy it.'

'I got it from Mrs Dwyer,' she said, in a little voice, 'and I wasn't hiding, except from the dog, 'cept when the dog chased me up the tree. I spat at him and I hissed and he wouldn't go away. You're a meanie, you are, not coming to chase him away.'

'I reckon you're silly,' he said, and lurched up ready to escape, yet anxious to make sure that he had asserted his mastery beyond doubt. She looked sweet and he felt physically awkward as if he had suddenly grown a couple of sizes too big for his clothes. It was confusing.

'Where are you going?'

'Home!' He waved his hands in the air, listening to himself with distaste. 'Can't go anywhere else, can I? You've made a real mess of my morning, haven't you? Mrs Farlow is going to tell Grandma that I shouted and shouting's rude. I don't want people thinking I'm rude 'cos I'm not. They're all going to look at me when I go up Main Street again. I'm sick of everybody thinking I'm rude because my name's Cameron. They're always getting me mixed up with my brothers. My big brothers are creeps.'

He slouched off along the beach. 'Nothing's nice for them; everything's got to be nasty.'

'Michael!' It was a plaintive cry that twisted at him, but he walked away from it.

The cliffs were only a few hundred yards away and Deakin Beach was round the other side. The tide was low. He'd be able to cross the reef on foot even though the rocks were tricky with mussel shells as sharp as knives and the pools were deep, with sting-rays on the bottom.

'Please, Michael.'

'Oh—get lost.'

66

The rain had stopped. When? He hadn't noticed. Perhaps he could spend a while paddling in the shallower pools before the tide came back, but his thoughts were scattered by the pressure of her presence crowding him. The squeal of sand under her shoes was so close he expected her toes to clip his heels.

'Haven't you got a home to go to?' he snapped, as someone once had snapped at him.

'I'm a witch. I just fly around. I told you.'

He pivoted irritably and confronted her at a range of inches, forcing his heartbeat into his throat. 'You're a nut. Why don't you go and pester somebody else?'

She looked tiny and forlorn, looking up. For the first time in his life he saw the face of a girl as something he wanted to touch and saw his hand go out to her as if it were part of someone else and control over it had nothing to do with him. He felt her take hold of it, felt sick from the shock of contact, then followed after her because she tugged on his hand in the direction they had been taking. He had not wanted that.

'Can I come home with you?' she said.

'I suppose so.'

Her hand was cool but his cheeks flamed.

'Yeh; yeh, Margaret,' he murmured inside, 'come home. . . . But what'll Grandma say? What'll the kids say if they see?'

He looked about guiltily, hastily, but the beach belonged to them alone.

He was shivering and felt prickly, as if a rash were breaking out under his arms. Those kids would tease him ragged if they saw. He'd never live it down. 'Whatcha doin' with a girl, Mick?' they'd say. 'Whatcha holdin' her hand for? Does she kiss good, Mick? She's a little kid, Mick. Can't you get one your own size?'

She was bustling along beside him with busy little steps, too short for him, making walking difficult. He was inches taller than her, but she was doing the tugging, almost pulling him along. 'Don't step so short,' he said, a little dismayed, because his voice sounded hoarse and cross and he didn't feel in the least bit cross.

Gravely, she matched her steps to his, long steps, like the kids who marched with their fathers in the Anzac parade, but the thought disturbed him and he tried to thrust it from his mind. What would Dad say? 'Never make friendships on impulse, my boy. We choose things we pay for with great care and friends are more important than anything we buy. Choose them, boy. Weigh them up. Because when you make a friend you give away part of yourself. It is only right that it should be a fair exchange.' He had understood what Dad had meant; Dad always made sure of that; but now it seemed so clinical, so cold, like the smell of ether in a doctor's surgery, like having a needle stuck in your arm to protect you from disease.

'Does she kiss good, Mick?' the kids would jeer.

He felt breathless, with a fire in his cheeks and smarting eyes and a tremble in his knees, but she dragged him along like a dog on a leash, chattering again now, chattering about all sorts of things that he hardly heard. But she was such a little girl. Was walking away with her committing a crime? She shouldn't have been on the beach at all. Would the police come knocking on his door !

'Look,' he said, 'look, Margaret. Listen to me. Where do you live? Where do you come from? If you don't tell me I can't take you home.'

'We're not going to *my* house,' she said, 'we're going to yours. Have you got a big house?'

'Big enough, I suppose.'

'Big enough for me to stay?'

'Crikey, I don't know about that.' His voice turned shrill. 'You can't do that, you know.'

68

'Don't you want me to come?' Her voice was shrill, too.

'Of course I want you to come.'

'Well make up your mind.' She sounded so *old*, as if their ages were the other way round. 'Are you rich?'

'Am I *what*?'

'Are you rich?'

He almost lost his stride. 'Of course I'm not rich. I'm only a boy.'

'I was sure you were rich,' she said. 'Then when you had paid my ransom I could have lived with you until Monday.'

His astonishment reduced his voice to a squeak. 'Your *ransom*? What the heck are you talking about?'

'Ten dollars,' she said, rolling her eyes as if ten dollars were riches beyond imagining.

'You only pay ransoms when you're kidnapped!'

'But I am kidnapped.'

He dropped her hand as if it had turned white hot and seared him to the bone.

'They poked me in the boot of a car,' she said, 'and then drove all night. They put me in a room without any windows and said don't move or we'll shoot. But I twisted my magic ring and turned into a mouse.'

'Come off it,' he wailed.

'They missed with their guns because I dodged and was so little. Then I ran out under the door. There was a splinter and it scratched my back.'

'You couldn't be kidnapped,' he said, sounding as unbelieving as he could, but all sorts of horrible thoughts were tumbling in his head and she bent over and pulled up her dress. The frilly seat of her pants, encrusted with sand, made her look like the tail-end of a rabbit. The scratch was as clear as day across one bony shoulder blade.

'See!'

'Put your dress down,' he cried. 'Do you want to get me run in?'

'There was a man called Spike and another called Michael. Michael had a patch over one eye. He was *nasty*. Now everyone will think *you* kidnapped me. When they get the ransom note everyone will think it's *you*, so it's best you pay the ransom before they come to get you. They *hang* you for kidnapping.'

'They do not.'

'They do too.'

'But I haven't kidnapped you.'

Her eyes turned into familiar huge circles. 'Who's going to believe that when they *all* come looking for me, blowing their sirens and throwing their tear-gas bombs?'

He couldn't make a sound. His lips turned into a spout, his tongue poked out, but not a sound was there. He could feel his hair, strand by strand, prickling on his scalp.

'I'll tell them you tied me up and blindfolded me and gagged me and wouldn't give me a drink or anything. I'll tell them you barked at me and chased me up a tree.'

Then she plodded away with long strides, almost as if she still held his hand, on towards the cliffs, looking ridiculous, and suddenly his voice poured out, hurting him. 'Tell them. I don't care. You're the one they'll be locking up. They'll lock you in a padded cell or something. You're stupid, you are. Who'd want to kidnap you? I bet if you were kidnapped they'd *let* you run away. I bet they'd say get out of our hair before you drive us up the wall. I bet they'd open the door and chuck you out on your ear.' Then there wasn't any voice left; it choked up with a croak and his brain was like a big ache.

They were singing another hymn, that mob up at the War Memorial. It *couldn't* have been the same one; sad and mournful it was, like a lost sound that had been wandering for years looking for someone to listen to it.

And Margaret was walking away.

Farther and farther she went, nearer and nearer to the cliffs, and something inside him began to tear.

'Don't go away, Margaret,' he said, but she didn't hear. How could she have done?

'Let her go,' Dad's voice warned. 'Remember what I said. Make a friend and you've got to give. Lose a friend and give again. It's only right there should be a little bit of take. Choose and think. The world's a tough place.'

But he didn't want to think. He was sick to death of worrying about reasons, about thinking and explaining. He wasn't giving anything to Margaret; Dad was all wrong; she hadn't taken a thing. It was the other way about. It came bubbling out of her and lay all around. She was stupid. She was a nut. But the tearing went on.

Margaret was not like the rest of the world to be weighed in a balance. She was taking nothing away except herself.

His feet flew over the hard sand after her.

'Hey! Wait!'

CHAPTER SEVEN

There were rocks in the sea at the foot of the cliffs. They looked like hundreds of people asleep, some on the sand and some in the water. Some looked like fat men with huge bellies, floating.

Margaret couldn't have known about them, that they were dangerous and slippery and that the pools were deep. It was terribly dangerous going out there, specially with shoes on. Little kids weren't allowed there unless they could swim like fish or had been taught by their big brothers and sisters exactly where to put their feet.

He raised an arm as he ran, sure that it should have called her back. Surely his fear for her was strong enough to reach her as clearly as words, but it wasn't. She didn't seem to care, just walked on to the rocks out into the sea.

'Margaret! Come back!'

Surely, to her, his thoughts should have rushed like sound waves across sand and sea and rocks, but they didn't. She was *separate* from him, farther from him than any stranger would have been. That was hard to understand.

He started yelling: 'Margaret! Don't go out there. It's slippery there. No, Margaret, it's deep.'

But she wouldn't listen and was still so far ahead. What had happened to distances? What had happened to time? Everything had stretched like a dream. He ran like mad and hardly dared think the thought that turned into the shout that drove ahead. 'There are sting-rays out there. Can't you hear? A little girl was slashed last summer. Ambulance men and hospitals and seventy miles an hour.'

She looked tiny against the great greasy sea and the broad grey sky and the looming brown cliffs.

'They had to stitch her up. She was sick for months. Margaret, don't go out there.'

She looked tiny enough to drown in an instant and he was her guardian angel. Of course he was. If anything happened to her it would happen to him too.

'You silly little creep,' he yelled. 'Come back.'

But she was *stubborn*. He floundered to the reef's edge thirty or forty yards from her and yelled again, 'Come back. Don't be silly.'

But still she picked her way seawards from outcrop to outcrop with arms extended for balance like a walker on a wire. She couldn't have been *that* stupid. 'You're showing off,' he cried. 'It'll bally well serve you right. You'll drown. Bigger people than you have drowned out there. It's way over your head.'

It was like one of Grandma's stories of a goddess walking into the sea to vanish beneath the waves. The rocks were like huge saucers out there, half-awash, almost as if they were floating and at any moment might sink or tip or spill her off. That blooming little kid, that crackpot. She'd got him so churned up he couldn't think straight, could think only of bodies floating in the water with long stringy hair waving back and forth like seaweed, could think only of people crying and an awful emptiness in the world. 'Oh, gawd,' he moaned and leapt out after her with leaping strides, cutting across open water to reach her sooner, certain that it was going to happen and it would be his fault and that if he didn't reach her in time he'd have to drown with her. 'Margaret,' he shouted desperately, then the shelving sand dropped steeply beneath him and the bottom wasn't there. Astonished that he could have forgotten, astonished that it could have happened, as the sea smacked over his head and a great gulp of sea-water flushed into him. 'I've got all my clothes on. I'll kill her to pieces. I'll shred her.' Then he burst up into the air, spluttering and coughing and spitting, half-blinded, completely bewildered, with not the vaguest idea of direction. Margaret he couldn't see anywhere. 'Margaret,' he bellowed, ejecting sprays of water, flapping around in a fever looking for her. Not in any direction. Nowhere. She'd gone. That poor little kid had fallen in.

'*Margaret!*'

That poor little kid. That poor little kid.

Something grabbed him by the hair and he thought of sharks and sting-rays and nameless horrors and fought against it. Handfuls of hair seemed to be coming out by the roots. A shrill voice beat against his ear, 'Don't worry, Michael; you're safe; I've got you.'

The heat of his panic turned to outrage. It was *her*!

'No,' he shrieked.

'I've got you.'

She had the nerve, she had the gall, she had the absolute cheek to imagine she was rescuing him.

'Let me go!'

'I'll save you, Michael.'

He dragged against her in a raging temper, wrenching his head with desperation, but she had a grip of total determination on his hair, and his scalp seemed to be peeling off in layers.

'*Let go.*'

But she wouldn't give an inch and eluded him like an eel. He struggled and twisted in a flurry of spray, trying to get his hands on her, but a set of sharp little knuckles arrived out of space and crashed against his nose. He felt the crunch, felt his face go flat, felt something like blank amazement and a sudden collapse of spirit. What

74

was the use? She was too stupid to understand the language.

Her legs started kicking vigorously—like a busy beetle upended—and salt water and misery poured into him and the tug on his hair was all the torments of hell. Sand met his feet and rock scraped his back and she puffed and blew and heaved and dragged him by the neck from the sea. Choking him. Almost choking him. The horrible strangling sounds he could hear were his own. She'd maim him for life. He'd grow old, a poor little man hobbling on a stick with his head twisted round back-to-front and Boy Scouts would help him across roads. 'What happened to you?' people would say. 'Arrrggghhh,' would be all that he could reply.

'No,' she said as he struggled to sit up and a wrench at his hair flattened him on his back. His head cracked down onto hard and rugged rock and stars sparkled all around. Her mouth came down to fill him with her breath, wide-open mouth like the gate to Luna Park, and enough breath to inflate him. He was horrified, outraged, and he came up kicking and clawing and yelling, 'Leave me alone, will ya?' and he rubbed frantically at his mouth because that was the end of all humiliations. But she returned to the attack and he could think of nothing but a tortoiseshell cat wearing a collar two inches thick with brass studs in it. In panic, he threw up the palms of his hands, pushing her away, fighting her off, shielding himself. 'What are you doin'' to me? Get lost, will ya? I'm not drowning, you little horror . . .' But the ache in his head hit him with spasms, and there were more stars in the sky than he had seen in the night. 'I'm all *right*! I can swim a mile with me eyes shut!' Getting the words out was like spitting up teeth.

'Margaret,' he cried, in final, frantic desperation. 'Lay off.'

75

Did it get through to her? Did she understand? Was she actually sitting away from him, squatting on her heels, looking like injured innocence? 'Strike me,' he moaned, 'they ought to lock you up.'

'You were drowning,' she said.

He bared his teeth.

'You were too,' she said.

'I was not.'

He rubbed his neck and nursed his head and panted for breath and couldn't believe that Michael Cameron was awake—or alive either. 'I can dive from a high board,' he said weakly. 'I can do freestyle and the butterfly and sidestroke. I can skin-dive. I can stay underwater for ages and ages.'

'Me too.'

'I've never drowned in my life.'

'Me neither.'

'Oh—*pigs!*'

He'd pull himself together and go home. Would he ever pull himself together? He'd get as far away from the monster as it was possible to get and forget she'd ever been born. He was so mad he could have spat. But then he tasted something and licked his lips and put his hand to his nose and stared at it, aghast.

Blood. Blood on his hand. Blood trickling from his nose.

'*You've blooded my nose,*' he shrieked.

She giggled.

'You little twirp!'

She looked sheepish, then giggled again.

'I'll clobber you if you don't shut up!'

She pursed her lips in a ridiculous fashion, like a fish, and made squirting sounds in her cheeks.

'To think I only came out to help you, to stop you slipping off the rotten rocks. Are you barmy or something? Can't you see if you fall in there you'll drown?'

The squirting sounds in her cheeks became a choking sound in her throat, and he snarled at her, completely missing the point. 'Why didn't you answer me? It's dangerous out here. You can't tell me you didn't hear. Anyway, if I'd drowned it would've been your fault. It's a wonder I'm not dead. And will you stop your silly laughing. Hasn't anyone ever told you not to laugh at people?'

She rolled her eyes instead.

'Pulling my hair out by the roots! What's wrong with you? It's a wonder I'm not bald.' He felt his head to make sure that he wasn't. 'And it's a wonder me nose isn't busted all over me face. What'd you bash me like that for?'

'You don't know anything, do you?' There she sat on her heels looking so superior he could have chucked a rock at her. 'To quieten you of course! You always hit people when you rescue them.'

'What a load of rubbish that is. Who told you that?'

'Everybody.'

'Well, everybody's crazy. And did you have to bang my head down? I'm not a lump of wood. I've got brains up there.'

'Goodness me,' she said, 'you're a grizzler, aren't you? I save your life——'

'You didn't!' His teeth snapped shut and he wagged an irate arm in the air. 'I could swim out to the channel where the ships are. All the way out there and all the way back. Yes I could.'

'You'd better not.'

'Why not?'

'You'd drown.'

'Turn it up,' he said unpleasantly. 'You've done that to death. And one more thing, too. What'd you go and kiss me for?'

'It was mouth-to-mouth,' she said. 'It wasn't kissing.'

77

'I hope not! 'Cos if that's what kissing's like I'll not be kissing girls, ever.' He shuddered to the pit of his stomach. 'I didn't need mouth-to-mouth and you bloomin' well know it. You only wanted to kiss me. I know what girls are like. I know all about them. I bet it was you who got that little boy into trouble at school. I bet it wasn't him at all. I bet you've got boys on the brain or something. I bet you're kissing and cuddling all the time.'

But she wasn't looking at him any more and her eyes were downcast and he began to feel cross with himself for raving on, not only because it made his head hurt, but because he didn't feel mad at all, not deep down, not any more. His temper was sitting on the top like a crust over something underneath that was nice. It was disturbing because he knew he was the one who wanted to cuddle up and do the kissing to find out what it would be like. She was terrific, but so little, so young. It wasn't right.

He grumbled to himself and mumbled and looked away but knew they were still scarcely a foot apart. He was four years older than her. Four whole years. He shot her a sneaking glance. There must be something wrong with him; he must be real sick like Mrs Farlow said; sex mad or something; except that Dad was six years older than Mum, and the grandfather he had never seen had been *ten* years older than Grandma. Crikey, Grandma had been *married* at sixteen. He shivered when he thought of that. Only seven years older than Margaret and *married* to a grown-up man.

He wiped blood from his nose on his sleeve and felt bodily uncomfortable, as if Grandma's God was visiting him with a plague because he had bad thoughts. But what could be bad about wanting to kiss a girl? Why did it have to be bad when you were thirteen but all right when you were grown-up?

He became more and more uncomfortable; sitting

there saying nothing; sitting there doing nothing. 'Does she kiss good, Mick?' the kids would say. 'I don't know. I didn't kiss her.' 'Why, Mick? Wouldn't she let you? You sat with a girl, *all that time,* and didn't get a kiss?'

Perhaps he would give her a smile to break the ice because he had been a bit hard on her, shouting and calling her for everything. After all, she had *thought* he was drowning and had made a jolly good job of rescuing him; if he had been truly drowning she might even have saved his life. For a little girl of nine and a half that wasn't bad, not bad at all. Maybe she'd taken a big risk; maybe she'd been very brave; perhaps she'd been feeling for him the same sort of things he had been feeling for her; perhaps she was sitting there right now, looking all pensive and shy, *waiting* for him. So he dropped a hand to his side casually, as if he hadn't noticed, and squirmed on the rock to make out he was trying to get more comfortable and came to rest with a leg touching her. The touch made him feel odd and shivery and slightly panicky. If she had objected he would have leapt into the sea in shame.

'Aw,' he stammered and tried to smile without actually smiling and to give her hand a squeeze without actually making contact. It was impossible of course and the suspense was agonizing and the shiver he had felt a moment ago turned into a visible tremble.

'Aw, heck!'

'What's wrong?' she said.

But he couldn't say. He was so ashamed. He was shaking all over.

'You're wet,' she said. 'It's bad for your weak chest. You'll catch a chill.'

'I haven't got a chill!' His voice was explosive. 'I haven't got a weak chest. I'm strong.'

'You don't look it.'

He grabbed her left hand and held to it fiercely. It

79

felt small and soft and submissive as if he had hurt it, and suddenly he dropped it. 'I'm sorry, I'm sorry.'

'Why?' she said.

'I didn't mean to hurt.'

'You didn't hurt.'

He turned his face away from her, sorely embarrassed, and folded his hands in his lap, shivering.

'I'm glad I saved you,' she said. 'It would have been awful if you had drowned.'

He shook his head, almost wearily.

'I knew you'd come though. All the time I knew. All the time I was walking away I was twisting my magic ring wishing for you to come. You were very slow.'

'I *ran*,' he said breathlessly.

'You shouldn't have had to. It should have happened in a trice.'

'What's a trice?'

'You know,' she said, 'wham, whoosh, bang. In a *trice*. I shouldn't have to tell you that. But you're little for thirteen. Phil's tall. Phil's my big brother. You don't believe, that's your trouble. Magic rings don't work for you. You're a septic.'

'I'm not.'

'You are.'

'I'm not.'

'Septics miss all the fun, my Mum says. They miss all the nice things, my Mum says, because they think they're clever and they're not.'

'I'm not a septic. I'm the very opposite. I'm just like you. Anyway, there's a "c" in it. It's sceptic.'

'You don't know what a trice is,' she squealed, 'and you try to tell me what a septic is!'

He grumbled to himself but wasn't unhappy. Something about it was nice and warm and natural. His shivering was going away.

'I'm sorry for you,' she said, 'not believing in magic

80

or anything. Mrs Dwyer's not going to be pleased if the salt water's spoilt my ring. She said it was the best she'd ever had. It'll be terrible if it doesn't work any more. *What*'ll I tell her?' Her eyes widened until he was sure they were the biggest on earth. 'Mrs Dwyer tried it out herself, she did. She wouldn't even *tell* me what had happened. "Ooh, Margaret," she said, "it's a *wonderful* ring." '

He took hold of her hand again, less firmly than before, pretending to look at the ring, but really to touch her fingers, hoping they might grip his own. But their worlds and their thoughts were not the same. She was too young; she didn't understand; and he felt ashamed. 'It's a beautiful ring,' he said, relinquishing her. 'Why don't you give it a twist? Wish for something.'

'No. You don't believe. You'd spoil it.'

He lied fervently. 'I do believe.'

'You don't. Mrs Dwyer said never use it when there's a *doubter* around. Or it might never work again. I wish you did believe, though.'

'I *do* believe.'

She shook her head. 'You don't. Phil doesn't believe either. He messes it up for me all the time. Phil's a septic too.'

Then she started pulling her dress over her head and for a moment of total confusion he tried not to notice, tried to make out it wasn't happening, then wailed, 'What are you doing?'

Her flushed face appeared like a flower in the midst of folds of brown velvet and pink underwear with inches of bare skin underneath. She looked startled. 'Taking my clothes off.'

'Holy cow! You can't do that!'

'They're wet! I got wet saving you.'

'You were wet before!'

'Not sea-water wet. Sea-water wet feels creepy. It

81

gets creepier and creepier all the time. I'm starting to itch. You take yours off, too.'

He could produce only a breathless protest and the dress went over her head all the way, dress and petticoat and singlet, then she shook out the creases.

'You shouldn't do that, Margaret,' he stammered. 'Put them back on, please. I'm in enough trouble around here.'

'Go on,' she said, 'take yours off, too. I don't care.'

'Crikey,' he moaned, and caught himself staring at her. She was separating the garments, laying them on the rocks. She didn't care, he knew that. 'Look, Margaret, you'll get me shot.' He turned his head away and faced the open sea, rubbing his nose and eyes and mouth with the flat of a fevered hand, smearing smudges of blood from ear to ear, terrified that her pants were going to come off next. 'Don't you understand you don't wear clothes in this climate just to keep warm! You've *got* to wear clothes. People get cross if you don't.'

'When they're wet?' she wanted to know in a high voice. 'My Mum gets cross if I *do*!'

'I'm not going to stay,' he said. 'I'm not. I'll go away somewhere if you don't put 'em back on.' His throat was sore with the heat of his embarrassment. Confusing images crowded him, grass and rain and Mrs Farlow next door, silly things he had thought and said. How silly they were. Dad would kill him. Dad would string him up by the toes. Holy cow; if anyone caught him with a naked girl!

'You're funny,' she said. 'Phil wouldn't care.'

'Phil's your brother!'

'Jesus says you're my brother too.'

'Arr! Come off it. Boys and girls don't get undressed in front of each other. You know that. It's not like wearing swim-suits. It's not like getting a tan. We'll get into trouble.'

'I'll turn into a cat if someone comes, if that's what you're worried about. No one cares if cats don't wear clothes.'

'Put 'em on again, Margaret!'

'They're wet. They're horrible. They're all wriggly.' She giggled. 'Aren't you wriggly, too? Aren't you all itchy? I know why you won't take your clothes off.'

'You don't.'

' 'Cos you've got pimples. 'Cos they're itching like mad and you don't want me to see.'

'I haven't got pimples!'

' 'Cos you're skinny then. 'Cos you haven't got any muscles.'

'I have got muscles. I've got lots of muscles.' He turned on her with eyes shut hard and dragged up his shirt sleeve and flexed his arm. 'See? Real muscle. I can do twenty push-ups off the floor.'

'Phil can do forty.'

'This bloomin' Phil gives me a pain.'

She giggled. ' 'Cos you're all hairy, then, like a monkey.'

'I'm *not* hairy.'

'Phil's got hairs. He's got *five* on his chest.'

'Bully for him.'

'Is that why you don't want to get undressed? Because you haven't got hairs on your chest?'

'*No!* I wouldn't have hairs on my chest if they gave them away free. And I wish you'd shut up.' He was shaking so hard it was like a pain.

'Why don't you open your eyes?'

'Because *why*, that's why.'

'I bet you're itchy.'

'I'm not.' But he was and every time she said the word he itched frantically more and more.

'You're funny,' she said, and giggled. 'Are you scared I'll look at it?'

'Look at what?' But with a horrible feeling of fright he knew. 'You're awful,' he yelled, outraged. 'Leave me alone.'

'You're a cry-baby, aren't you? Go on, why don't you cry?'

He wanted to hit her; wanted to hurt her; because he had thought she was different from everybody else and she wasn't. She was the same, she was worse, she was a girl. He bared his teeth at her and raised a fist and met her face to face. She still wore pants and shoes and socks and looked so pretty and suddenly a little bit scared. He dropped his arm and moaned, 'Don't tease me.'

But she was scared and started gathering up her clothes.

CHAPTER EIGHT

She was going. It was awful that she was scared because
he would have died before he would have hurt her.
Surely she must have known his fist would not have
struck her, would never have gone all the way. He
shook his head and stammered a bit but she was a girl
and he didn't know about girls and had no idea what
to say. She shouldn't have teased, not after the happy
things they had shared.

Please stay, he wanted to say. *I don't care about your
clothes; I know I'm being silly. I don't care about the things
you've said, even. It's just that I was surprised.* But he couldn't
put it into words. *It's just that I'm frightened of what
people think. Other people never seem to understand. They
make things nasty and they're not nasty at all. And I forget
that you've got brothers and you're used to boys. But I'm
different from Phil; don't you understand?* But thinking and
saying were not the same.

'I can swim,' he blurted out. 'I can. I wouldn't tell
fibs to you.'

She had her clothes in her hands and had gone yards
towards the shore gingerly on her way, not looking
back, trying to balance without the aid of her arms.

'I can swim. Don't you want to see?'

He tore off his shirt and kicked off his shoes, kicking
them into the sea, and plunged from the reef with an
enormous, clumsy splash, then cut sleekly down seven
or eight feet to the bottom rolling as a porpoise might
have done and it was ecstatic to be free of itches, to be

85

eased and soothed and calmed, it was terrific to be the master of his body and nerves. His shoes, waterlogged, drifted like lazy fish to be captured and he burst to the surface with one in each hand. 'See,' he shrieked and pitched his shoes to the rocks, at once somersaulting, not waiting for her approval, not even bothering to check whether she had seen, and cut again towards the bottom, contorting himself, twisting, gliding, showing off until he would have fainted without air.

He burst up, flicking hair from his eyes, spouting like a whale, even though sharp movements of his head were not achieved without pain. She wasn't there.

'Margaret. . . . You didn't go. . . .'

He could have sunk and stayed down. Despairing, he crawled on to the rocks, up where it was dry, water streaming from his clothes.

'Gee, Margaret. . . . Why?'

As soon as she had hit the sand she must have raced into hiding where the tea-tree grew. How could she have been so frightened? Had he twisted his face in some horrible way, baring his teeth more horribly than he did at other times? Kids at school sometimes said, 'Heck, Cameron. Fair go. Pull your fangs in.' But then in an instant of joy he saw her clothes scattered as if forgotten or put aside. He stood up casually, trembling, as if he had known all the time, almost sick with happiness, and there she was on the inside of the reef, lying down, as if reaching for a shell that might have been submerged.

He wanted to call but didn't trust his voice to convey the right tone. It might break or turn harsh, it might sound cold and destroy the miracle that had made her change her mind. But she stayed there unmoving and looked strange and something welled up in him with concern.

'Margaret! What are you doing?'

She didn't move, didn't answer, and his sudden fear

became a stammering cry. He leapt across the reef, terrified, not understanding. How could anyone like her suddenly be so strange?

Death was the fear. She looked dead; that's why her clothes were thrown. She had slipped because he had said she would, slipped because her shoes were still on, slipped and struck her head? Slipped and now dead. He fell to his knees and dragged her from the edge of the sea, hair-ends floating like string. She was as limp as a doll made of rags. Lifeless and limp. With a mark above her eyes, those beautiful eyes closed, and water spilling from her hair, with a head that rolled. He crushed her against himself. He cried and didn't know what he said. Then he put her down and sat beside her holding her hand, the one with the ring, stunned.

Who was Margaret Hamworth? They wore bags of camphor. Where had she come from? Oh, the great big hole in the world where she had been.

Where was he to take her? What was he to do?

They'd say, 'How did it happen, boy?'

'She fell. Can't you see?'

'Why did it happen, boy?'

'She was running away.'

'From you?' they'd say.

'I don't know. Why should she run away from me?'

'Who was there with you, boy?'

'No one else. Just us two.'

'You should have taken care. She was little. You must care for the little ones. Why did she run away from you?'

'She was funny. She was so funny. I didn't know from one moment to the next what she was going to do. She said she was a witch. In a trice, she said, she could spirit herself away. But I wouldn't have hurt her. I wouldn't have hit her. She shouldn't have teased. Golly, Mr Policeman, I know what you're thinking, but it just isn't true. . . .'

He didn't want to think any more.

No more. No more thinking. Thinking was an awful place. Awful things became more awful there.

'How did you come to be with her, boy?'

'I don't know. It was just like she was there. It was Mrs Farlow's rotten old perfume. She said she was a cat but I'm not the Michael who kidnapped her. If there's a note it's not me. It's some other fellow with a patch on his eye. I didn't kidnap her. I didn't. I've never seen her before. I didn't.' Her hand was stirring and he gave it a squeeze. 'I didn't do anythin', Mr Policeman, I didn't, I didn't.'

Her hand was alive.

He seemed to shiver inside his veins and could scarcely see her for his tears. But she was blinking at him. She was moving all over like a puppet stirring to life, a wonderful, extraordinary thing, as if she had come back from death, as if he had been reprieved at the instant the door on his own life had been clanging shut with panic. A hundred horrors melted away, all the nightmares of having to explain to grown-up people who'd never quite believe. Oh, the relief that Margaret was still something alive and warm. He was sitting her up, he was hanging on to her, he was saying 'Margaret' over and over again. He was saying, 'Oh, Margaret, I'm so sorry you fell; I wish it had been me. Oh, Margaret, you know I wouldn't hurt you. You didn't have to go away. I'm your friend. I even like growling at you. I'm even happy when you're teasing me; really I am. I don't care. You can say anything you like to me. I don't mean it when I shout at you. I want you to be my friend. I want to see you all the time.'

'You're funny,' she said, and he suddenly became shy, as if perhaps he should not touch her any more. He held her arm politely, steadying her, and in a little while she said, 'Goodness, did I fall down? Was I—*unconscious*?

I've got an ache. Is it a headache? I've never had a headache before. Was I—*unconscious*?'

'Yes,' he said.

'Really and truly?'

'Yes.'

She thought about it, with thoughts flickering like lights on her face. 'Goodness, and I don't even remember. Fancy being unconscious and not knowing. Was I unconscious for long?'

'I don't know. A minute or two I suppose.'

'Not an hour or anything?'

'Not an hour. No.'

She pulled a long face, with a pout and a roll of her eyes. 'Wasn't much, was it? Only a minute or two? Are you sure? That's hardly worth it, is it? Not for a day or anything?'

'No.'

'I don't think much of that. Rosemary was unconscious for *two days*. I thought when you were unconscious the doctor had to come. Didn't he come? Weren't there any nurses or anything?'

'No,' he said, and smiled, feeling good again. 'Just me.'

'I'm sore. Am I bleeding like you?'

'No, you've got a lump.'

'Only a lump?' She touched it with her fingertips, tenderly. 'Only a miserable lump? It's a *big one*. You've got blood everywhere. You're real gory, you are. Did you have a fight or something? Was it a shark? Did you get unconscious, too?'

'No, of course I didn't!'

'Ooh, and you were swimming. What if the sharks had come? Ooh. . . .'

'The sharks didn't come!'

'All that blood and the sharks didn't come? I wouldn't swim with all that blood. They'll bite your leg off. P'raps they'd bite your head off and then what'd you

89

do? Ooh. . . . You were going to hit me, weren't you? You raised your hand to me. That's why the sharks came. Jesus sent them to punish you, because I'm one of his sunbeams I am.'

'*The sharks didn't come!*'

'Oh yes they did. You can't fool me. I know. Have they gone away now?'

'Yes,' he sighed, 'they've gone,' and pulled his wet singlet off and used it to wipe his face clean. He had forgotten his nose-bleed; he had forgotten it would bleed for probably an hour. The Cameron nose was famous. Every time someone took a poke at it! He should have been holding his head back with ice-bags slapped to his brow.

'You won't hit me any more, will you?'

'No.'

"Cos I'll tell Phil if you do.'

'I didn't hit you before.' His mouth began to droop again at the corners.

'But you were going to. Your face was *ugly*. You've got a bad temper you have.'

'I haven't.'

'You have. That's a sin, that is. You're a sinner you are.'

'You're a nut!'

'Are they your friends?'

'Who?'

'Those boys. I'll tell them you were going to hit me. I'll tell them you kidnapped me. I'll tell them you made me unconscious. I'll tell them you don't believe in magic rings or anything. I'm cold I am. I'm sore. I've got a lump on my head. I've never had an ache in my head before. . . .'

They were crossing the beach perhaps a quarter of a mile away where the lane came down from the War Memorial. There couldn't have been too much wrong with her head if she could recognize them as boys. The stride of the big one, the tall one, was the swagger that Bruce MacBaren put on when he was feeling tough and was looking for a bit of sport to liven up his day. One had to be Flackie and the other was Ray Farlow.

Michael didn't hear her prattling; nothing she could say could make it worse now. Bully Boy and Flackie were horrible enough. Horrible. But why did it have to be Ray as well? Ray was supposed to be going to a football match. If Ray came his Mum would hear the lot, the whole miserable tale, and it would be all over town in an hour. Mick Cameron and a little kid of nine with a bruise over her eyes. Mick Cameron with a bloody nose. 'Mick Cameron,' they'd say. 'Well, we're not surprised.'

It was too late to do anything now. Too late to run. Too late to make up a story anyone would believe. They were yelling and waving their arms. They knew and had seen.

CHAPTER NINE

What was the use? Nothing ever went right for Mick Cameron. Couldn't say boo to a little kid of nine without turning the world upside down. All the fretting and rage and exasperation that he had secretly enjoyed had emptied out and left him frightened and cold. 'Gee, Margaret,' he moaned, 'look at the trouble you've got me in now.'

But she didn't hear; she was chattering on ninety-to-the-dozen. You'd have thought a crack on the head hard enough to knock her flat would have quietened her down. But it was only something to prattle about! Didn't she care? Didn't she know? It must have been great to be nine-and-a-half with not a worry in the world.

He closed his eyes with a shiver, to shut Bully Boy out, to shut out Flackie and Ray, wishing desperately for the beach as it had been only a few moments ago, wishing for a bolt from Heaven that would sweep the three of them back to the War Memorial in a swirling willy-willy of sand, but Bully Boy was leading his procession along the edge of the sea. Swaggering along. Why did they have to pick on him all the time? Why couldn't they leave him alone? Why couldn't the sea rear up and drown the so-and-so's? Trouble like sickness always came when Bully Boy brought a crowd. He played it that way.

'Hey, young Mick,' he'd say, 'tell us a joke. Make it dirty and I'll let you off.'

But Michael couldn't remember 'dirty' jokes. They always fled from his mind.

'Hey, young Mick,' he'd say, 'do us a cartwheel.'

But Michael never could. His cartwheels always went wrong, ending in a heap on the ground, one arm or the other giving way.

'Hey, young Mick,' he'd say, 'try to punch me in the jaw.'

Bully Boy, in the mood for ritual, sounded like the TV shows that Dad turned off with a flick of the wrist and a scowl. 'Tripe.' But it wasn't tripe when it was real. When it was real you didn't know what to do. You couldn't switch it off.

The procession was coming along the hard seaside sand with a real tough stride and Michael wanted to run all ways at once, a little bit of him here, a little there, hundreds of pieces that would never be found. He couldn't bear it, the things they'd say, making him a fool in front of her. But he couldn't run; he couldn't let her know he was scared—because Phil wouldn't have been scared. Phil would have poked 'em in the nose! Phil would have done this and Phil would have done that. Blooming Phil would probably have stood there biting on his nails, squirting fire from his ears.

She was gathering up her clothes again. She was not in any hurry, wasn't worried, didn't care. Gathering them up and chattering all the time. In pink pants. From the distance they'd think she was starkers. Probably think he was, too, and he tried to wriggle back into his singlet and remember where he had dropped his shirt but it was yards and yards the other way, and he didn't want to leave her, didn't want to give her the chance to get away. If she started blabbing her story as she was telling it now he'd end up in gaol. 'You can't say those things,' he croaked, with a voice so brittle it was a wonder it produced a noise at all. 'You're talking fiddle-faddle. You know you won't say things like that because they're not true. If you're one of Jesus's sunbeams he'll be cross with you for tellin' lies.'

'Don't you call me a liar.' And she was off again; holy cow, she was off again; she must have been plugged into a radio station for continuous sound; he wouldn't have been surprised if she had started playing music like a band. And all the time his own thoughts ran frantically on: *They're going to tear me apart. They're not like me, Margaret, you know, not when Bully Boy's around. He's real tough, that big one; he's nearly fifteen. You won't be able to give him the push the way you've pushed me. He'll put you back in your box; he'll slap you down. But what's wrong with bloomin' Ray? What's he doing with kids like them? Ray was my mate for years and years. Look, Margaret, we've got to get out of here. I can't fight three. I've never won a fight yet that wasn't a game.* But thinking wasn't saying.

'Hey, young Mick,' Bully Boy was shouting, sticking to the ritual. It'd go all the way, maybe not to blows, but to shame. Bully Boy would break him down with words and he'd be so flummoxed he'd have to run. *Go to blazes, Bully Boy. Can't you leave me alone?*

'What have you got there, young Mick? Are you playing with the little kids now?'

What could you do? What could you say? Bully Boy had his crowd but Mick Cameron was alone with a little kid of nine stuck on a heap of rock in the sea. He'd have to get to Deakin Beach, somehow, but the tide hadn't been going out, it had been coming in. Maybe he could wade, but maybe he'd have to swim. And what did he do with her? Leave her behind to blab, or cart her off home like something he had found?

Go away, Bully Boy. And Margaret was looking at him, looking a bit odd. Her chatter had run out, dried up, gone dead. He had thought she would have made a break for the beach, but she stuck close, hugging her heap of clothes like an orphan of the storm.

'It's not a girl, is it, Mick?' Bully Boy yelled. 'Wow. Where'd you get her, kid? Steal her out of a pram?'

'I don't like him,' she said.

'They run you in for baby-snatching, young Mick.'

'You shut up, Bully Boy,' he shouted. 'You hold your tongue.'

'Easy does it, kid. They're crook on you back at the War Memorial. Screaming your head off when everyone's sayin' prayers. They won't reckon on getting you for baby-snatching as well. A baby all bare, hey, Mick?'

It was surprising how far they still had to come, but Bully Boy had a voice like a trumpeting elephant. Ray half-waved an arm, as though he wasn't sure of his ground, as though he'd rather be somewhere else. Kids were like that when Bully Boy was around.

'Your mate's here, aren't you, Ray? He says his Mum's real crook on you, showing her up. Ray's crook on you, Mick. Don't you run away, young Mick. You've got to come with us. You've got to bring the girl, or her father'll chop your head off. He's real crook on you.'

Bully Boy was in good form. He wasn't soft-pedalling because of any little girl. If there was fun to be had he'd be in for his share and Margaret seemed to know. Her hair was drooping from the roots, bedraggled, and she was hugging herself as if the air had become wintry and cold. Her changes of mood were bewildering him more because she seemed to be taking his side. Michael had seen her lined up with them, as his accuser, as a chatter-box not caring for the trouble she'd cause. 'Come on,' he stammered, 'we've got to get home. Round the cliff. The other side.' But because that sounded so weak, so awful, so terrible, he added with a jerk of his thumb, 'We can't be bothered with *them*. They're crumbs. They're not our kind.'

'If he comes too close,' she said knowingly, 'I'll turn into a cat and scratch his eyes out. He's rude, saying things like that about me.'

'I'm not going back with them, see; I'm not goin''

anywhere with 'em. . . . And suddenly he was fiercely impatient with her and himself and the whole wide world. 'Come on,' he said roughly.

'Where?'

He pulled her with him into the water, dragged her after him, and dropped with fright to chest depth. Her head was scarcely clear. She looked terrified and seemed to be suspended vertically bouncing on her toes, water flooding to her chin like something bent on choking her. He had expected it to be less deep. Here they were not far from the shore.

'My clothes,' she wailed.

'Blow your clothes.'

'I'll lose them. I can't swim with my clothes. I'll drown.'

'You swam with them before.' Why was the silly little drip so small?

'I was wearing them then.'

'What'd you take 'em off for?' he snarled. 'I told you not to.'

'I don't want to go. I don't want to go.'

'You'll do as I bloomin' well say.' He snatched her clothes and dragged her with his free arm, but she struggled and broke away.

'Don't you go back,' he yelled. 'You come with me.' She swam ahead of him, swam on, and he waded in her stream, and Bully Boy, Flackie and Ray had come to the shore.

'What are you running for, young Mick?'

'I'm running nowhere,' he shouted over his shoulder. 'You leave me alone.'

'You won't get far, young Mick. Her Dad'll be coming after you.'

She was over the deep patch, climbing up through the water-worn boulders into the shells and shallows under the cliff. He waded after her with face set grim, with not a thought in his head that he could understand. For two pins he'd have tossed it all in and swum out to sea, out and out to where the big ships were and people could never pursue.

'Push on,' he urged.

She looked frightened and confused. 'Why are we running away?'

'We're not.'

'Aren't we?'

'No, I said; we're not.'

'We'll get you, young Mick. Running won't help. We're coming.'

But they weren't; they were still standing on the shore.

He shouted at them, 'I'm not running. If I want to move I can, can't I? It's a free country. Push off. Leave us alone. Pick on kids your own size.'

'Gee, Mick,' Ray yelled, 'we're not picking on you. You ought to hear the others. You ought to hear that little girl's Dad. Mum says you've got to go home to bed.'

'Yeh, young Mick. She reckons you're silly in the head with the flu. She reckons you're too stupid to come in out of the rain.'

'It's not raining,' he yelled angrily, 'and I haven't got the flu.' Then he snapped at Margaret, 'Go on, push on. You're dragging your heels.' And, after a moment, 'You don't believe them, do you? They'd say anything.'

'Hey, Mick, you'd better tell her to put some clothes on or her Dad'll chop your head off. Have you been swimmin' in the raw?' That was Flackie, laughing. Flackie gave him the creeps. Flackie gave him the horrors.

The cliff pressed at their sides like craggy-legged giants, knee to knee, soaking their feet in the water.

'What was it like swimmin' with her, Mick? Did you have fun?'

97

He tasted blood again and wiped it from his face on his shoulders.

'Hey, young Mick. If you don't come peaceful I'll have to catch you.'

'Yeh, Mick, we'll have to catch you.'

'Her Dad will be after you, Mick. He'll dong you with his trumpet.' Even Ray was joining in now.

'These blooming shells,' Michael complained, but it wasn't far to the sand. His nerves were like glass because she had shoes on and he didn't. He didn't have shoes at all; or a shirt. He'd left them somewhere behind. All he had was an armful of clothes to fit a little squirt of a girl. Hugging her clothes, losing his balance, stumbling all the time. Deakin Beach, like a crescent deserted and golden, was coming into view.

'You're not scared of those bullies, are you, Michael?'

'No, I'm not.'

He had got ahead of her and jumped from the rocks into the shallows and Bully Boy wasn't there any more, cut off by the face of the cliff, left behind. His voice was left behind, too. All their needling voices were gone. Margaret splashed in after him; the sound of her wading was there, but he wouldn't look back at her, didn't care, and plodded up onto the beach, grumbling to himself, sniffing, even spitting coarsely because he felt the need to be rough and rugged. He felt so puny, so ashamed.

The brown cliffs hung over him. The zig-zag steps were there. The leafy street where he lived was up on top, back from the edge a hundred or so yards, not to be seen from down here, only to be imagined. Grandma was up there, too, in her room that smelt like a cave. Holy crackie, Grandma. The things that happen to me.

'Punch them in the belly, my Mum says, and they run away.'

'Punch who in the belly?'

'Bullies.'

98

He was mad with her and still wouldn't look at her and was straining his hearing for sounds of Bruce Mac-Baren. He pulled his socks off, wincing, and felt like a stranger to himself, felt lost, felt awful, felt a shockin' awful failure. And she'd been unconscious, hadn't she? There'd been no fib about that. He'd been terribly rough with her. What would he do if she flaked out again? 'Your Dad's in the band,' he scowled, 'isn't he? Or he wouldn't have a trumpet. You should have told me he was in the band. You should have told me he was a Salvo. I could have taken you back to him ages ago. I suppose he told you to wait up on the road or something and you wandered off. You're lucky it was me that found you and not someone else. You're lucky you didn't get into serious trouble.'

'He hasn't got a trumpet. He bangs the drum. He bangs it with a big stick with a knob on the end of it. He might dong you with that.'

'He's not going to dong me with anything. Why should anyone dong me? Why should he?'

''Cos you kidnapped me. You've kidnapped me now, haven't you? *You made me come with you*. They saw. They'll tell.'

'You're a nut.' His upper lip twisted but he wasn't really caring; he was watching too anxiously for Bully Boy, knowing there was no hope at all of beating him to the top of that cliff, of scrambling safely home. It was not a moment to be bothered with the stupid things she had to say.

'If we're running away,' she said, 'why are we stopping here?'

'Strike me, we're *not* running away.'

'Where's your house?'

'On top of the cliff.'

'Well, why don't we go there?'

'Because we're not running away!' He snapped his

99

teeth together, but felt like a jelly. 'You don't think they scare me, do you?'

Would Bully Boy come round the foot of the cliff or over the top, blocking the way home? Would he lose interest and not come at all? It was an awful, jittery, scattered sort of feeling. All because of her! Then she moved in front of him and interrupted his view, though he tried to ignore her, stupid girl in pink frilly pants.

'Put your clothes on!' He tossed them at her but she let them drop.

'They're wet.'

'I said put them on.'

'They're *creepy*.'

'So what! So are mine! Haven't you got me in a big enough stew? Can't you see this is all your fault? Why didn't you say your dad was in the band? Why didn't you tell me? I didn't know who you were. I thought you must have lived here somewhere. You stupid little girl.'

She shrugged in a most annoying way.

'You should have waited in the crowd for him. You shouldn't have come down to the beach. Now what do I do? There ought to be a law against girls. Telling me you were a witch. It was Mrs Ellis's terrier, anyway, spot or no spot, I knew all the time. Hiding when I wasn't looking. Who did you think you were fooling? You couldn't turn into a cat for a million dollars and I wouldn't believe you if you did.' He had to suck hard or he would have dribbled from rage. 'Put your clothes on!' He could have hit her; he really could have done. 'It's all right for you, you can go away, you can go home; I've got to live here and put up with it for the rest of me life. Those kids'll never let me forget it.' He tried to hold the outburst back, tried to get on top of it, but couldn't. 'All you do is get me into trouble. You're a fibber. You're a little sneak. It was going to be a real beaut day and now look at it! Why don't you take off?

Why don't you go *pooff* or something? Why don't you get lost? You give me a pain.'

But she stayed on, drooping in front of him with a trembling mouth, with the part of her he had known sliding away from him like a shadow over the sea, melting into nothing a long way off. A stranger was left, of no importance, recently met for the first time, an ordinary little girl of nine like thousands of little girls of nine, about as interesting as last year's geography.

He wiped his nose on his arm and drew more blood. 'Go on, push off.'

She cried, but her tears meant nothing. He couldn't have cared less. Dad was certainly wrong. There was no 'exchange' for good or for bad. There was nothing. She might as well have never happened.

'You're not fair,' she murmured, 'going on like that at me. I'll put my clothes on; I'll be good; I won't be any trouble. I'm scared. I don't want to be left alone.'

'You've thought of all that a bit late, haven't you?'

'I like you, Michael. I saved you. I want you to look after me. Phil's not here to do it.'

He was drawing sharp breaths, one after the other. 'You didn't save anybody. You live in a dream. *You* save *me*! You saw me swim. I can swim rings round you.' He swept his socks up from the sand and scowled at his blood-stained singlet, perhaps scowled at everything in the world. 'Look at m'clothes; what's left of them. Look at *me*. Grandma'll throw a fit. How'll I explain?'

She started scrambling into her dress, getting everything tangled and back-to-front, but he headed across the beach for the zig-zag steps that would take him to the top, one hundred and ninety-three steps up. And it looked like he'd get there; Bully Boy hadn't come; Bully Boy must have given it away. 'I'm off,' he said. 'I'm goin'.' Was it relief or what was it? Was it astonishment that Bully Boy hadn't come? He sighed as if knots and tangles in his stomach had come untied. 'I'm off. You can do as you please.'

She groped after him with a button of her dress snagged in her hair. 'I'm *caught*.'

'Don't come that with me.'

'Michael,' she cried, 'it hurts. . . .'

'Too bad.'

A movement startled his eye and his heart skipped a beat as a rock as big as a football came bouncing down the cliff and thudded into the sand.

Up there at the edge, hand to the rail of iron, was Bully Boy looking a mile high, the way the cliff used to look when Michael was little and Mum was alive.

'Get a hold on her hand, young Mick, and we'll take you back to her Dad.'

CHAPTER TEN

Then it was Flackie who came to the edge, grinning. Michael couldn't see the grin, but no one had to tell him it was there. Flackie looked like everything that Michael despised.

Then Ray came. In his Boy Scout uniform. Ray should have been ashamed. A Boy Scout up there with merit badges and all. Ray Farlow in that sort of company. It was a crying shame. Ray mightn't have been perfect but he was not that sort of boy. *Crumbs, Ray,* Michael moaned to himself, *it's not fair. I'm still the kid I used to be. What could have changed? I can't believe you'd turn on me.* Then he felt the alarming physical contact of a stumbling little girl.

'My hair's caught. Don't be a meanie, Michael. Get my hair out for me, please.'

He was aware of her, grotesquely, with fingers groping oddly out of sleeves in the wrong places, with a brown velvet heap like a woman's crazy hat enveloping her head. The sight and shape of her offended him, her antics upset him, and in a state of distraction he pushed her aside, but blindly she found him again.

'Go on, Mick,' yelled Flackie, 'take it off for her.'

She was crying.

'Go away,' Michael hissed at her. 'I'm in enough trouble. Can't you see!'

'Are you coming up, young Mick, or have we got to come down?'

It was awful. Home was up there. It might as well have been a million miles away.

'Michael, my *hair*.'

'Shut up,' he pleaded, 'go away. I can't do it now. They're up there!'

'I'll take it off for her,' yelled Flackie, and maybe he was coming down. Maybe they were all coming down, Ray too. Zig-zag steps in an untidy pattern, some made of wood in flights gaping over holes, some cut out of rock, zig-zagging on the cliff face. They were coming down. But it was Flackie whom Michael feared, suddenly Flackie.

'You'll leave her alone,' Michael shouted threateningly.

Somehow, somehow he had to stand up to them or she'd think he was a coward.

Bully Boy was following Flackie a few steps behind; Ray was lagging more, but he was coming, like something on a chain, like something that couldn't get away.

He wanted a rock to throw, something harder than words, but there was only the stone that Bully Boy had dropped over the side; too big, too big; and the pebbles in the sand were all too small.

'She's not taking it off, anyway, she's putting it on.' And incredibly he found himself standing over her with his concern for her welling up again, wildly and possessively.

'Why don't you kiss her, Mick?' Flackie yelled.

'You shut up, Flackie. You get lost. You come down here and I'll smear you all over the place.' But he didn't feel brave, only frantic, and he was fumbling to free her hair, but couldn't. He was hurting her; she was crying; he was tugging. 'I'm sorry, I'm sorry, I'm trying not to hurt.' It was awful having to hurt her when all he wished for, desperately, was the courage to protect her. He was all thumbs and blunt ends and the stupid dress was in a knot on the top of her head. Three boys were zig-zagging down the steps, quickly coming.

Flackie looked like something that should have lived in a hole under the ground. Bully Boy looked as big as a man. Ray, like a louse, trailed them down.

'Her Dad'll chop your head off, Mick. Won't he, Bruce? Won't he, Ray? Fancy catching the Duke messin' about with girls.'

He stumbled with her along the sand, pulling her, guiding her. He had thought that Deakin Beach was safe from the world, but it wasn't, it was a trap, like a lane in full view, too narrow for concealment and with fences too high to climb. He couldn't go up the cliff-face as he had done once before, not with her hanging to his arm.

She was crying, 'My hair. . . .'

'Hey, young Mick. Wait on. We can't give you a hand if you run away.'

Dad *wrenched* at sticky bandages and had them off in an instant too brief to hurt. The button was between his fingers. Somehow he found it there and on impulse he wrenched and she shrieked with pain but the dress fell from her head to the sand. She was gulping for air, her face was flushed and streaked with tears. 'It's off,' she sobbed and looked about four years old. 'Michael, why are they chasing us? Why are we running away?'

Did he know? Did it matter? He grabbed her by the hand and forced her to hurry, but was scared for that head of hers, scared she might faint.

'My dress,' she cried. 'I can't leave it there.'

But he dragged her along with floundering strides, in a panic, seeing nothing except the rocks at the far end of the beach a fifth of a mile away, huge boulders tumbled from the cliffs in a heap by time, fantastically pitted by wind and sun and storm.

'My clothes,' she cried.

He ran with her, dragging her along behind.

There, among the rocks, he'd let them know who was

who. There were rocks and stones and driftwood from the bay, things he could fight with, things he could throw. There, maybe, he could show even Bully Boy a thing or two.

'Michael,' she sobbed, 'my *clothes*.'

He could hardly get his breath and it was so difficult running through sand with a dead weight on the end of his arm. She was so heavy, she was such a drag.

When he got there he would make his stand. It was so far away! He would fight Bully Boy tooth and claw. Bully Boy would be sorry he had ever been born, he'd paste him, he'd plaster him, he'd kill him. Flackie, too. That kid he'd punch raw, he'd break his teeth, he'd smash his jaw. There were things Dad didn't understand, things Dad had forgotten. How could you fight things like Bully Boy with words? You fought with fists and feet and knees and nails and lumps of rock, like a savage. Dad had medals in his drawer. Did he get them for waving books in the air?

'Stitch,' she cried and doubled up and almost pulled him down, but he dragged brutally, refusing to let go. The rocks were not far, not far, but she was a great weight dragging on him through the sand; it was like trying to pull a tree, like sinking into mud with despair. The rocks were so far; it was such a shame. There was a hole inside him contracting his body, a huge hole out of which all flesh and hope had gone. He fell on his hands and knees with blood running from his nose again and she dropped somewhere near him making a funny sound like a squeaking wheel.

He could have cried.

It was like the end of the world, like failing in everything he had ever tried to do; like dying, only worse, because maybe with dying that'd be the end. Being like this meant there was more. It was terrible being alive. Why couldn't he be dead like Mum, like those ten million fellows who had marched off to war? Thinking exhausted him; half-thinking, half-feeling; it made him want to cry, made him want to die.

They were there, through a haze, Bully Boy, Flackie, and Ray.

It had happened. He had always known it would. They were there.

Pieces fell from him into the sand, grains of strength, drops of blood, streams of sweat. He couldn't have struggled up if he had tried, could barely hold himself as he was, down on his knees, with the button of her dress still pressed in his palm, with strands of her hair caught between the fingers of the same hand. Wearily he wondered why he could feel them there, but they were important, they were terribly important, and he tried to glimpse her, moving only his eyes, but she must have been somewhere behind in the haze.

'I told you not to run, didn't I? You're too delicate, young Mick, for violent exercise. You've got yourself a bloody nose.'

It was Bully Boy, and Michael struggled to calm himself, even to surrender, to go numb so that nothing could hurt any more. What was the use of trying to hold on, or run farther when they had arrived? Dad was in Canberra, Richard and Gregory were far away, and Grandma was in her room that smelt like a cave. He was alone and no one cared.

'Gee, Mick,' Ray said, 'Mum's mad, but not *that* mad. She's worried in a way. You put on such an act. She says I've got to take you home to your Grandma and make sure she puts you to bed.'

His head sagged and the words went over the top of him; he let them go. They were only a lie. Ray had been slinging taunts like the rest of them. Ray had been in it for his bit of fun.

'She's a cute little bird, isn't she?' Flackie said. 'But

where'd she get the bump on the head? Has he been fighting you, kid? That'd be his style, fighting a girl. Your Pop's the bloke in the band, isn't he?'

'Come on, Mick,' said Ray, 'don't muck about.'

'You'll bleed to death, young Mick. Get your head back. You haven't got the blood to spare.'

Margaret came edging against him but he saw only her back sparkling with sand, like something made of sugar that would last for an hour, then melt, then vanish. Sitting there; sitting against him; leaning; possessing. He could have shrunk from her touch but she had made contact and wasn't going to lose it. Why couldn't he have got to the rocks? If it had not been for her he'd have made it with yards in hand. He'd have been there now fighting like a savage. He'd have spilt blood and not cared. He'd have aimed rocks to hit. He'd have fought. They'd have known that Mick Cameron had taken all the lip he was going to stand.

'You shouldn't be playing round with fellows like him,' Flackie said. 'He's always chasin' girls, bigger ones than you. He's got a real bad name.'

He could have taken Flackie by the throat.

'Come on, Mick, be a sport. I've got to get back to Mum and Dad.'

He wanted to sneer at Ray, to wither him; that was all that Ray was worth; he wanted to tell him exactly what he thought of him.

'Yeh, Mick,' said Bully Boy, 'get up before I drag you up by the hair. We're missing out on our lemonade.'

Force hung over Michael like a threatening weight, but didn't fall.

'If they go to the footy match without me I'll be crook on you. Dad's cranky enough now. If he changes his mind it'll be your fault. Come on, Mick; what are you doin' down there?'

Three pairs of legs still standing, with voices going

plaintive, as if they were looking to each other for help with things to say, as if for some reason or other not one was game to make the first move. Michael tried to think around it, tried to work out why. Did the two of them look so terrible, so sick lying there, that they were *afraid*?

'He's a real bad egg, kid,' Flackie said. 'We could tell some things about him, couldn't we, Ray? Everyone knows about Mick, don't they, Ray?'

'Yeh, yeh; but put another record on, Flackie.'

He was aching on his knees, drooping in the small of his back, sniffing blood and tasting it, getting cold. His sweat was turning into something like frost, but three pairs of legs still stood like a fence in the sand. It was stupid, it was crazy, but Michael couldn't drive himself to move. Nothing of his body would answer any call. It was a dull feeling, dull, like lying in the sun on a hot afternoon, except that it wasn't hot, except that it was cold, except that she was there.

'Gee, Mick, come on! We've got things to do! What are you doin' on your knees?'

'Saying his prayers,' said Flackie. 'God bless Daddy. God bless Mummy. God bless me.'

'He hasn't got a Mummy. Don't be cruel.'

'Strewth, she talks! I thought she was clockwork. I thought she'd wound down.'

'I'm going,' Ray said, sounding awkward, and for all that Bully Boy had had to say he might as well have gone too. But Ray didn't go, his legs bent a little, but stayed. 'Plug your nose up, Mick, for crying out loud. Stick a cork in it or something. You'll bleed to death. Is he in a trance?'

Margaret was becoming restless, stirring against him, perhaps wanting him to move, perhaps wanting him to fight. She was the only touch of warmth there was, the pressure of bare skin against his side. Could he go through it again, that wild scramble, running like mad, dragging

109

her behind, reeling into the rocks, grabbing lumps in his
hand, aiming and throwing? 'No, Mick,' they'd scream.
'Stop it, Mick. Do you want to lay us out cold? We'll
go away.'

'Maybe he's her slave,' Flackie said. 'You know, like
in the olden days. Why don't you kiss her foot, Mick?'

'Shut up, Flackie. For Pete's sake!'

'Yeh, what's eating you, Flackie? Leave her alone.'

'Strike me pink; who's talking now?'

'I am,' shouted Bully Boy. 'Leave her alone.'

'Leave her alone? Have you gone pure or something?'

'I don't pick on nice little girls.'

'Who's picking on *nice* little girls?'

'You can see she's only a kid. Are you trying to scare
the daylights out of her?'

'Hell's bells. What's she been up to with him? Looks
good, don't it? Runnin' like smoke. What'd he run away
for? You said it yourself, you crumb.'

Could *that* be Flackie? Had he gone round the bend?

Michael lurched away from her, lurched up, lurched
to his feet almost drunkenly, feeling sick from having his
head down too long. He couldn't see much, everything
swam. He couldn't think much, everything was slurred,
words and thoughts and feelings were mixed up with his
feeling of sick. Flackie was there but not steady, as if not
in one place. He could feel the blood draining from his
head until his legs gave way and he remained upright
only by kneeling again and by digging his hands into the
sand. Ray was running. Yes, he was. The big Scout was
running home to his Mum. Bully Boy was looking angry
or odd, looking awkward, as if something had gone
wrong.

'Flackie.' Michael knew he said the word and knew
what was coming next. It came, as if he spat it out. He
didn't care any more if he got hurt. 'You stink.'

Flackie took three strides, four strides, five, and

Margaret shrilled, 'I'm a cat. I'll scratch your eyes out. Don't you touch me.' Then Flackie's hand came flat and open and pushed Michael in the face.

He lay on his side in the sand, sprawled, and the beach was a haze of lines and levels and shapes with human figures on it like splashes of paint, Margaret scuttling away, yards away, Bully Boy swaying like a brush stroke back and forth, Flackie taking his raincoat off, fumbling with the buttons, tearing it off. 'Stink, do I, Mick Cameron? I'll show you who stinks.' Flackie was all spite, he had been sick in the head all his life. And Flackie was coming for him. Flackie would tear him to pieces. There'd be nothing left for Bully Boy to torment.

Michael reared up with a cry and there was nothing to see but Flackie and Flackie was all the rotten things of life that he couldn't run away from any more. He threw himself blindly and hopelessly and their bodies met, a collision of flesh and bone and dread.

It was a mad spasm that went on and on and on. It wasn't like seeing or feeling or hearing separate things, it was like getting drowned in a raging flood under the earth, in a storm drain miles long where everything was violent and roaring and dark. It was awful. It was terrible. It was wonderful. It was like breaking out of prison into space.

Michael was standing in the sea with his feet apart, with water swelling over his ankles, swelling to his calves, then sliding past, and the roaring in his head was going, throbbing away like a ship out of sight. His fists were unclenching, his muscles unknotting, his lungs were reaching for great gulps of air.

He was standing on his feet and something had happened. His singlet was torn from top to bottom, there were scratch marks on his arms and thighs, he ran a hand over his face and it came away blooded, there was a pain in his side. He remembered none of it, had felt none of it, but stung to it all now. Flackie was huddled in the water, heaped up like something thrown away, heaped there, sobbing.

Michael Cameron had won.

He had fought and won.

He wasn't crying. He wasn't running. He hadn't lost. And it wasn't only Flackie down there, it was Bully Boy and all the sports-masters and prefects and Smart Alecs at school. It was even Mrs Farlow and Ray. He had taken from all of them all that he could stand. They'd know now, every one of them, even if he never breathed a word. There were some things he wouldn't have to say; he'd wear this like a badge. They'd see it for themselves. They'd know.

He waded from the sea onto the sand and took possession. He had owned it by right and secured it by strength. Yeh, Dad, *resisting* aggression. Flackie stayed huddled in the sea like a heap of weed.

Ray had gone. Clear out of sight. Up the zig-zag steps, over the crest of the cliff, he'd still be running half-a-mile on the other side. Blooming Ray. What would he say to his Mum and Dad? 'Couldn't find Mick anywhere. Didn't see him at all. We'll be late for the footy if we don't get started now.' Did Ray see how it had ended? Did he wait on the cliff? Did he know?

It was strange standing there with an arm pressed to his nose, peering over it as though over a wall.

Bully Boy had gone to drink his lemonade. Bully Boy was thrashed even though his body wasn't left lying around. 'Couldn't catch them up,' he'd tell the man in the band. 'If you want your little girl, mister, you'll have to find Mick Cameron. He's the kid who'll know.'

Disappeared like magic; like rabbit-in-a-hat was his middle name. Had Bully Boy waited long enough to see?

Margaret had gone, too.

He flopped on the sand, hugging his knees, swaying

112

a little from side to side. Flackie's sobbing sounded like the sea.

She'd gone.

With Bully Boy? With Bully Boy who didn't pick on nice little girls? Bully Boy with his glossy red hair and his deep voice, nearly fifteen.

'Holy cow, Flackie. Don't cry like that.'

Bully Boy was tall, like Phil. Bully Boy could easily do forty push-ups off the floor.

'I'm a witch,' Margaret would say, pacing beside Bully Boy, stretching her strides to match his. 'Michael doesn't believe in magic rings. Do you? Michael's stupid, isn't he?' Yeh; that's how it would go. 'You haven't got a weak chest, have you? Michael has. Do you know what he tried to tell me? Doesn't know what a trice is and that septic's got a 'c'.'

Only Flackie was there. Everyone else had gone; the game had been played; they'd all gone home.

Did Margaret know that he had fought for her? Did she care? Was this the way it was with wars? The people you fought for not caring. Did you fight for nothing? After it was over did they all go home, not looking back, shrugging it off, forgetting that you weren't the same any more? Did you thrash people who lay down and cried? What were they crying about? Would you ever know?

Flackie was coming up out of the water, almost on his knees, and Michael wanted to say, 'Look, I don't care. It could have been the other way.' But all he could do was stare, as if Flackie couldn't be hurt by staring and had no feelings of his own. Flackie hung his head and walked in the direction the others must have gone, trailing his raincoat behind. What would Flackie say when he got home? Something, for sure, because he looked as if he had fallen from a train. 'I got in a fight with a big kid,' perhaps he'd say. 'Must have been sixteen if he was a day. Picking on the little kids he was. I taught him a lesson or two.' Yeh, Flackie would get out of it, he'd cover up, he'd manage.

Flackie shuffled farther and farther away, looking horrible, looking like he'd been broken and didn't want to live another hour. It was sad, somehow.

He'd have run after him, he'd have said, 'Don't feel bad, Flackie, it was only words,' but it didn't happen because Flackie veered off towards the sea and looked back along the deserted beach to where Michael possessed the world. Perhaps he glared, or sneered, or cried. Then he scooped two objects from the sand and threw them away from the shore. Perhaps they were the socks that Michael had worn. It was a shame he did that. He shouldn't have done it. It was a terrible shame. In a while when Michael looked again Flackie had gone up the steps, home to his Ma and Pop.

'Where are your clothes?' Grandma would say. 'Your shoes, Michael, your socks, your shirt? For Heaven's sake, child.'

'I forgot them, Grandma, when I was playing a game, and the tide carried them out to sea.'

'There's blood all over you, Michael. Why?'

'I got a nose-bleed, Grandma, from sneezing all the time, from that rotten old perfume Mrs Farlow wears.'

'But does that account for your singlet?'

'Torn, Grandma, on a tree.'

There'd be so much to explain.

'You're scratched. Scratches, child, everywhere.'

'Yeh, Grandma, the tree.'

'And wet. Your trousers are soaked through and through.'

'From trying to get my clothes back, Grandma. I must have swum a mile.'

Viciously, he pitched a handful of sand into the sea.

Margaret should have stayed. Margaret should have stayed. Why did she go away?

'Please, Grandma, what's the sense of it, being on your own all the time, even when you're the winning side?'

How could she understand if he wouldn't tell her why? He'd never tell her, never.

'If this is how you come home, Michael, when you go off alone, I think next year we'd better go together to the Anzac parade.'

'Next year, Grandma? Who cares? What about this year? What about today?'

He wouldn't say that either; it was half-baked. He didn't know what he'd say; she was so old.

He was kicking the sand, weaving, stride across stride, up and down. You could walk a mile when you wanted to and get nowhere at all. The beach was empty and he wished for the Lindens and the Bischofs and the Olsens of the summer time. Brian was a terrific kid; even his sister Wilma wasn't bad in a boyish way. Could he swim? Could he make that marathon swim out into the channel, way out there? Could he swim beside the ships down the harbour to where the ocean began? Some other time.

Margaret's clothes had gone. She had picked them up, she had really gone, truly gone, no more hiding, no more silly stories, no more Margaret.

She was so little; she didn't understand.

Ray was sitting at the top of the steps, huddled. He had changed into knock-about clothes and looked so miserable it was a wonder he didn't burst into tears. He wanted to say something, that was clear, and had two or three tries while Michael stared. 'Dad's changed his mind. . . . He's staying with the fellows. . . . I've got new stamps. . . . Gee, Mick, I didn't know what to do. . . .'

Ray followed a few yards behind. 'You killed him, Mick. You really killed him.'

'Yeh.'

'Mick, I'm sorry. . . .'

After that Ray fell farther behind. Maybe tomorrow. Maybe next week. Maybe then.

CHAPTER ELEVEN

He turned the shower on until it ran hot, as hot as he could take, then stepped under it not undressed and everything swirled down the plug hole into the earth, grains of sand, sea-water salt, sweat and blood, all swirled away like bread-and-honey crumbs washed off.

He dropped his pants and rubbed them clean with soap and stood in a man's world of steam like a fighter in a Turkish bath. Stood there and stung; hot-water pebbles raining on his back.

Grandma was at the bathroom door, banging on it with something that sounded like a brick.

'Michael, I can't get in.'

'I know. The door's locked.'

'Why, for Heaven's sake? Come out of the shower and let me in.'

'I'm not finished, Gran. I'm not ready yet. If a fellow's in the bathroom a lady's got to wait.'

'I'm your grandmother.'

'What difference does that make?'

Perhaps she went away, or perhaps waited while the hot-water pebbles scarified his flesh.

'Michael.'

'Yes, Gran.'

'Are you ready yet?'

'In a minute.'

'Did you know we've overslept? *Today* we've overslept. It's nearly twelve o'clock.'

'Yes, Gran.'

'I've not missed the march in forty years.' Her voice sounded thin.

'You've missed it this year, Gran. It's happened. You can't put back the clock.'

'That's not like you, Michael, saying things like that.'

'It's a fact, Gran, isn't it? What's the use of dressing it up?'

He wrapped a towel round his waist and tucked it in securely and lifted the latch. There she was, still in her nightdress, hearing aid plugged in, all eighty-three years of her ('Oh, Gran; what lies under that skin?') with a wreath of leaves and chrysanthemums, green for heroes, white for sorrows, and red for love. There were tears in the furrows of her cheeks.

'Don't take on, Gran. It's all right.' He gave her a kiss and tasted salt. 'It's not too late for the wreath. The War Memorial's still there. It's a day for forgetting, anyway, same as for remembering, I guess. We'll go together, if you like. Just the two of us. I'll wear my best suit. How about that?'

He padded to his room holding up the towel and felt a stare on his neck. That had been the question of course, the one he had tried to ask a year or two back as Grandma had stepped out of the crowd to place her wreath, 'Is this because people remember, Grandma, or to pretend that they don't forget?'

About the Author

Ivan Southall was born in 1921. He was sixteen
when his first article was accepted by the
Melbourne *Herald*. He then wrote some thirty
stories and articles which were published all over
Australia. Ivan Southall served with the R.A.A.F.
for five and a half years during the Second World
War, beginning operational flights from Britain in
1943. He was awarded the D.F.C. in 1944. In 1945
he was posted to the War History Section of the
R.A.A.F. Overseas Headquarters, London, to write
a portion of the history of the R.A.A.F.

Ivan Southall has since become well known, both
in his own country and overseas, for his biography
of the Australian war hero, Bluey Truscott, his
account of the exploits of Australian mine disposal
officers in Britain during the war, *Softly Tread the
Brave*, and for his many award-winning children's
books.

He now lives in the Dandenong Ranges, near
Melbourne, and concentrates on writing for young
readers. He says he 'enjoys writing for children
more than any other activity'.

*Some other books by Ivan Southall,
available in Puffin editions, are
described on the following pages*

Hills End

There was no indication on that sun-drenched morning that the little Australian timber town of Hills End was doomed. Yet while most of its people were on a picnic and seven of its children were searching near-by caves for aboriginal drawings, the sky 'became glazed over with a bronze sheen', a cloud 'reached out of the north like a black arm and closed its hand round the sun', and the dark waters of the river flooded over the rock pan between town and hills.

When the children had struggled back to Hills End they found it deserted and destroyed. Surrounded by wild mountain and forest country, threatened by a flooded river, an escaped bull, and a shortage of food, they were faced with the problem of survival till help came.

This is an absolutely riveting story, full of suspense, which will appeal especially to boys over ten.

To the Wild Sky

Everyone was waiting for the engine to stop. It was bound to run out of fuel some time. The six children seemed to have been sitting in this plane, imprisoned, for days, waiting to die. And Gerald, who had taken over the controls when disaster struck their pilot, just flew on and on, almost as though he didn't know how to go down. Tomorrow was his fourteenth birthday, but he hadn't much hope of seeing it.

And if they did land, where would it be? On the mountains? On the sea? Somewhere near habitation, or in the desert wastes or even in New Guinea, where the savages were? It would take a miracle now to save the party who had set off that Friday afternoon to visit a sheep station in New South Wales.

Four boys and two girls, six different people, how would they stand up to this terrifying situation? Who would be a good leader, and who would crack under the strain? Would they work as a group, or would their disagreements kill them all?

For readers of eleven and over.

Finn's Folly

The car had gone away. There was nothing now, except mist in the hills . . . and Max, Brenda, Tony and David (David who was different from other children) were left alone in the holiday shack at Lakeside, waiting for their parents to return.

The semi-trailer had pulled out of the city back loaded with chemicals . . . it went grinding through hills and valleys at a steady fifty on the flat. *Speed it Thru Mac*: that was the sign on top. Alison sat beside her father in the cabin, dozing . . . until suddenly she jolted awake, pitched hard against her safety belt as the truck shuddered to a stop. 'Sorry, Love,' her father said, 'I've got myself lost.'

Fog. A country road in Australia. A hairpin bend. These are the circumstances out of which Ivan Southall weaves his moment-by-moment narrative of a single night when five young people and five adults are involved in a drama of life— and death. To each of them, until that night, a road accident was something that happened to other people. But when Max, Brenda, Tony and David, Alison, and Frank and Phyllis Ashford find they are actually involved in the aftermath of tragedy, then the real impact is made clear.

For readers of eleven and over.